Dear Reader,

I just wanted to tell you how delighted I am that my publisher has decided to reprint so many of my earlier books. Some of them have not been available for a while, and amongst them there are titles that have often been requested.

I can't remember a time when I haven't written, although it was not until my daughter was born that I felt confident enough to attempt to get anything published. With my husband's encouragement, my first book was accepted, and since then there have been over 130 more.

Not that the thrill of having a book published gets any less. I still feel the same excitement when a new manuscript is accepted. But it's you, my readers, to whom I owe so much. Your support—and particularly your letters—give me so much pleasure.

I hope you enjoy this collection of some of my favourite novels.

A. Mather

Back by Popular Demand

With a phenomenal one hundred and thirty books published by Mills & Boon, Anne Mather is one of the world's most popular romance authors. Mills & Boon are proud to bring back many of these highly sought-after novels in a special collector's edition.

ANNE MATHER: COLLECTOR'S EDITION

CAROLINE

BY
ANNE MATHER

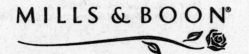

MILLS & BOON®

MILLS & BOON and MILLS & BOON with the Rose Device
are registered trademarks of the publisher.

First published in Great Britain 1965 by Mills & Boon Limited
This edition 1998
Harlequin Mills & Boon Limited,
Eton House, 18-24 Paradise Road, Richmond, Surrey TW9 1SR

© Anne Mather 1965

ISBN 0 263 80571 9

Set in Times Roman 10 on 12 pt by
Rowland Phototypesetting Limited
Bury St Edmunds, Suffolk

74-9805-53543

Made and printed in Great Britain by
Caledonian International Book Manufacturing Ltd, Glasgow

CHAPTER ONE

ADAM STEINBECK strode swiftly through the swing glass doors of the Steinbeck Corporation Building in Park Lane. A big man with broad shoulders, dressed in a dark suit and a sheepskin overcoat, he looked powerful and assured. As he paused for a moment to light a cigar, his keen eyes surveyed the reception hall. At his entrance, apart from the usual 'Good morning, sir' from the porters and female receptionist, an uneasy hush had descended and with a wry smile Adam acknowledged them before crossing to the lift. He was quite aware that the moment he was out of sight, a telephone call would hastily be put through to his suite of offices to warn his staff of his presence in the building. He rarely came in during the morning, but today he wanted to see Mercer and get those contracts wrapped up.

He stepped into the lift and was about to close the gates when a young voice called: 'Oh, please. Wait for me!'

Frowning slightly, Adam saw a girl rushing across the hall towards him. He got a swift impression of long, straight, fair hair, almost white hair in fact, a tall slim body dressed in a dark blue duffel coat, a shoulder bag swinging from one hand.

It was obvious from her manner that she was unaware of his identity and the hall staff looked agitatedly at Adam who moved his shoulders in a slight, deprecating gesture and stood aside for the girl to enter the lift.

'Oh, thank you,' she gasped with a smile, looking up at him with a pair of eyes which were incredibly green.

Adam closed the gates. 'Do you work here?' he asked, realising that she was probably an employee of his, although as it was almost nine-thirty, she was obviously late.

'Yes,' she replied, trying to get her breath back. 'I work in the typing pool. Miss Morgan's domain. Do you know her?'

Adam half-smiled. His rather dragon-like senior in the typing pool had always amused him.

'Yes,' he answered, 'floor three, I believe.'

'That's right. I'm awfully late and I'll get into such a row, but honestly, we never heard the alarm this morning and Mandy said she was sure she had set it last night.'

'Mandy?'

'Amanda Burchester, the girl I share a room with. Two rooms actually and it's supposed to be a flat. Amanda is an apprentice window dresser at Baileys.'

'I see.' Adam found himself strangely attracted to this young woman. She was such a refreshing change from the women of his acquaintance, and not recognising him she spoke freely and without any ulterior designs. Of course she was very young, probably about eighteen, but charming nonetheless.

'I haven't seen you before,' she continued, looking up at him. 'If I had I should have remembered. All the boys I know are my height themselves. I'm five feet seven, you know, but you make me feel quite small.'

'Thank you. I believe this is your floor.'

'Oh, yes. Gosh, it would be just like me to go straight past.'

'I wouldn't let you do that,' he said smoothly.

'Do you work here, too? Are you late as well? I've only been here two weeks, so of course I don't know everybody yet.' She stepped into the corridor.

'Yes, I work here,' he replied with a wry smile. 'I trust you won't have too much trouble with Miss Morgan.'

'So do I,' she averred fervently. 'Well, goodbye, then. I may see you again some morning.'

'You may, indeed,' he said easily, and closed the gates, firmly pressing the button for the top floor.

His office suite was accommodated on this floor, along with the offices of his co-directors and the imposing board room. He had his own staff of typists and his personal assistant, John Mercer, was in the adjoining office. The corridor here was thickly carpeted and all the rooms were soundproof and luxurious.

He entered the outer office of his own domain and saw that his private secretary was diligently typing as though unaware of his arrival. Laura Freeman was thirty and had been with him for over ten years. She always looked bandbox fresh and wore her long dark hair piled on top of her head in a neat knot. Whereas the rather severe style made some women look austere, with Laura Freeman it merely enhanced her good looks, giving her a businesslike air. Adam was well aware of her personal feelings for him but could not find any appeal in her himself. Their relationship remained strictly businesslike, much to Laura's chagrin.

As he closed the door now she looked up and upon

seeing him she rose to her feet. 'Why, Mr Steinbeck,' she exclaimed as though surprised at his appearance. 'We didn't expect you in this morning.'

'Come now, Miss Freeman,' remarked Adam, crossing the room to his own office. 'Surely reception hasn't slipped up for once. I could almost hear the wires tingling as I rode up in the elevator.'

Laura remained unembarrassed, and refused to rise to his baiting.

'The mail is on your desk,' she said in her most correct manner. 'Shall I bring in my notebook?'

'No, don't bother, I'll ring when I want you. Oh, and Miss Freeman, get me Miss Morgan on the phone immediately please.'

'Miss Morgan in the typing pool?' exclaimed Laura.

'Who else?' said Adam easily, entering his office and closing the door firmly behind him. Caroline Sinclair sat drinking her morning coffee with a fellow typist, Ruth Weston. It was ten-thirty and the typing pool staff were allowed ten minutes for their coffee break. Ruth was smoking, but Caroline was sitting staring thoughtfully into space, her shoulder-length hair framing her piquantly attractive face.

'Penny for them,' remarked Ruth, bringing Caroline back to earth abruptly.

Caroline smiled. 'Oh, I was only wondering why Miss Morgan was so understanding this morning. I've only been late once before and that time she was furious about it. Today she simply said she knew what it was like with alarms and that I should hurry and catch up with my work.'

Ruth, who was nineteen and two years older than Caroline, raised her eyebrows. 'Heavens,' she exclaimed. 'You've only been here a fortnight and I've never known her understand about anybody sleeping in before, let alone a new girl. Maybe she's got herself a man at last.'

Caroline giggled. 'Ruth, if she could hear you! By the way, that reminds me, I came up in the lift with the most gorgeous man this morning.'

Ruth looked interested. 'Really?' she said. 'How old was he?'

'Oh, in his thirties, I'd say,' replied Caroline blandly.

Ruth chuckled. 'Rather older than you,' she remarked dryly.

'So what!' exclaimed Caroline. 'I prefer men to boys. Boys always bore me.'

Ruth shrugged. 'Well, you know best about that, I suppose. What was he like anyway? To look at, I mean?'

'Oh, big and broad and very attractive,' murmured Caroline, smiling. 'Thick black hair cut very short and he was wearing one of those short sheepskin coats. He was what I call a real male.'

Ruth laughed. 'Honestly, Caroline, you must be joking, talking like that about a man who's probably old enough to be your father. Mark Davison should be more in your line. He's trying to date you, isn't he?'

Caroline grimaced. 'Ruth,' she exclaimed, 'Mark Davison is just an overgrown schoolboy, and is he big-headed! He thinks he's God's gift to women.'

Mark Davison worked in one of the adjoining offices in the building and had dated most of the girls in the typing pool from time to time, including Ruth. Caroline, being the new girl, was now being subjected to the treatment, but she was not interested and all the other girls were amused at Mark's persistence.

'Well, anyway,' went on Ruth, 'who was this man? Where did he get out of the lift?'

'I don't know. He stayed on after I'd got off,' answered Caroline. 'Do you know all the men who work here?'

'No, not all,' replied Ruth. 'There are too many different departments. I know a lot of them by sight, of course.'

Caroline nodded thoughtfully. Suddenly an imperious voice broke in on their conversation.

'Miss Sinclair, Miss Weston, I think your break should be over by now.' It was Vera Morgan on the warpath and with hasty steps the two girls returned to their machines.

The small flat which Caroline shared with Amanda Burchester was in an old converted mansion standing in a cul-de-sac off the King's Road. Once the home of a titled lady, the house now accommodated twelve separate couples and no children were allowed, although the scratched paint and peeling wallpaper had seen much better days.

Caroline's parents were dead, having died in a car crash when she was three, and she had been brought up by an elderly aunt. When Amanda had the chance of this flat six months ago, she had invited Caroline to share it with her, and Caroline herself had been very keen. Aunt Barbara was a dear old soul but not good company for a teenager, and she had been very understanding and allowed Caroline to go. Caroline had known Amanda since their schooldays and sharing a flat was great fun.

Although Caroline was less effusive, Amanda had a steady stream of boy-friends, some of whom gravitated to Caroline after meeting her. However, her height deterred many, and in any case, the boys who often appealed to Amanda did not often appeal to Caroline. Amanda was a redhead and eighteen years old. Her parents lived in the North of England now and as Amanda had not wanted to leave London when they did she and Caroline had acquired this flat.

Boys were only of secondary importance to Caroline. She loved reading and visiting art galleries. She attended most of the exhibitions and revelled in learning about the artists. She also enjoyed classical music and Amanda could never understand how she could dance madly one evening and then go into raptures over Grieg's Piano Concerto the next. She occasionally visited the Festival Hall when some famous musician was playing, but in the main she had to be content with the concerts on the radio, as after paying her keep at the flat she had very little left to do anything with.

When she woke up one morning about a week later and padded to the window she found a thick fog outside probing at the panes. Drawing the curtains quickly closed again, she groaned inwardly. Then she looked at Amanda, who was stirring, disturbed by the light that Caroline had switched on.

'Come on, Mandy,' said Caroline sleepily. 'There's a peasouper outside, and goodness know how long it will take us to get to work.'

Amanda rolled over in her twin bed, rubbing her eyes.

'Oh, dear,' she moaned unhappily. 'I feel terrible, Caroline.'

'Don't we all,' remarked Caroline, making a face at her, and crossing to the wash basin she began to clean her teeth.

'I'm serious,' exclaimed Amanda in a croaky voice, lying back on her pillows. 'I think I've got 'flu. I always seem to get 'flu in November.'

Caroline sighed and hastily washed and dressed. 'Are you going to work, then?' she called as she filled the kettle in the minute alcove off the living-room which served as a kitchen.

'I don't think I can,' replied Amanda miserably. 'Oh, Caroline honey, make me some tea and put a drop of that cooking sherry in it, will you?'

Caroline smiled at this, but went back into the bedroom and switched on the electric fire.

'Okay,' she agreed. 'Now, give me your hot water bottle and I'll refill it for you. I'll have to hurry, though, or I'm going to be late.'

'Never mind,' groaned Amanda. 'Nobody can expect you to be on time this morning. Besides, you might meet your dream man again.'

Caroline chuckled. 'Oh, Mandy, you're incorrigible!'

When the kettle had boiled she filled the hot water bottle and made the tea.

'Do you want anything to eat?' she shouted to Amanda.

'No, just some aspirin,' replied Amanda rather

hoarsely. 'I expect I'll be all right if I have the day in bed and dose myself like mad.'

'Well, don't overdo it,' said Caroline severely. 'I'll try and get home at lunchtime to get you something to eat.' She brought in the tea. 'Where are the aspirins?'

She left the flat a few minutes later after making sure that Amanda had everything she needed. She had not had time to have any breakfast herself and had had to make do with a cup of tea, gulped scalding hot.

Outside it was bitterly cold. The fog cast a gloom over everything and the thought of the winter months ahead was not a pleasant one. She joined the queue at the bus stop, but all the buses were so full that they did not stop and she realised she could probably have walked there in the time she had been standing, freezing.

At last a bus did stop and she was squashed inside. The bus crawled along. The traffic was congested and the fog was so thick that the driver could hardly see at all.

She reached the entrance to the Steinbeck Building at nine-forty-five and thought with a sinking feeling that she might really get the sack this time. After all, this was the third time she had been late and she had not been there a month yet. It was no joke, and she walked into the reception hall feeling very small and rather scared. Today there was no sign of the handsome stranger whom she had half-hoped to see and Miss Morgan was just as angry as Caroline expected. Caroline had hardly got through the door before she pounced and stood staring at her grimly.

'Do you realise, Miss Sinclair,' she stormed, 'that

this is the third time in as many weeks you have been late?'

'Yes, Miss Morgan,' Caroline managed to say, shakily. 'But I'm afraid the girl I share a flat with has developed influenza, and I couldn't come away and leave her without making her some tea and filling her hot water bottle.'

Miss Morgan was not impressed.

'Save your excuses for the personnel manager,' she replied icily. 'I intend to report you this time. I won't have such lackadaisical behaviour in my department. It's getting quite out of hand.'

'But, Miss Morgan. . .' Caroline began.

'Say no more,' commanded her superior. 'You've wasted quite enough time already. Kindly go and get on with your work.'

Caroline went to her desk feeling near to tears. She saw Ruth looking at her sympathetically but hadn't the heart to acknowledge her. The fog also did not seem to be thinning at all and she dreaded the rush she was going to have at lunch time, rushing back to the flat to attend to Amanda and then getting back here again, all in an hour.

She was summoned to Mr Donnelly's office at eleven o'clock. Mr Donnelly was the personnel manager and when Caroline met him at her interview she had thought him very kind and pleasant. Today, however, he was far from pleasant. After hearing a tirade from Vera Morgan he felt justly annoyed and the suggestion that his judgment had been lacking when he hired Miss Sinclair irritated him immensely. He was thus in no mood to be his usual amiable self.

'You realise, Miss Sinclair,' he snapped angrily,

'that I could fire you for this! You've let everybody down, especially me. It was in my power to employ you or not to do so. Having done so you go ahead and ridicule my recommendation!'

'Oh, no, sir,' exclaimed Caroline. 'I truly am a punctual employee in the normal way. It's simply that my flatmate has developed 'flu and I had to attend to her before leaving home. And then the fog. . .'

Donnelly strode up and down restlessly. He wanted to believe this girl with the honest eyes. He was almost convinced she was telling the truth.

'You've placed me in a very awkward position,' he said at length. He sighed heavily. He could see how distraught she looked and how she genuinely seemed to want the job.

'Very well, then,' he decided slowly. 'I'll give you one more chance. Any deviation from regular times after this will mean instant dismissal. Do you understand?'

'Yes, sir,' Caroline's heart was heavy. How on earth was she to manage at lunch time? She was tempted to ask him whether the might be permitted an extra quarter of an hour for lunch, but decided against it. He had been very fair and that would probably have been too much, even for him. As for asking Vera Morgan, that was unthinkable!

Back at her desk she did her work automatically, mentally calculating the time required to do what she wanted to do. An hour would just not be long enough. It would take her nearly half that time to get home, if she was lucky enough to get a bus, and as for getting back. . .

Ruth was frankly amazed when Caroline explained

that she intended going home. She was quite sure that Caroline would never make it and Caroline wondered whether she ought to develop 'flu too, and not bother going back at all. At least they couldn't fire her for that!

Ruth went off to the staff canteen at lunch time where both she and Caroline always ate in the normal way, while Caroline almost flew down the stairs, not waiting for the lift. She rushed across the hall and out of the glass doors. The fog did not seem so thick, but it was bad enough. In her haste to reach the bus stop, Caroline ran full tilt into a man coming from the opposite direction.

'Gosh, I'm awfully sorry,' she began, and then as he steadied her she stopped. 'Why, it's you!' It was the man from the lift.

He released her and smiled.

'Miss Sinclair,' he said easily. 'I am right, aren't I?'

'Why, yes, but how do you know my name?'

He shrugged and ignored the question. 'You're in an enormous hurry.'

Caroline realised she was wasting time and grimaced. 'Yes, it's too long a story to tell you now, but I nearly got fired this morning and now I'm taking my life into my hands again. I'm sure to be late.' She sighed heavily.

Adam Steinbeck hesitated and then he said: 'Perhaps I could give you a lift.'

'A lift?' Caroline was incredulous. 'In a car?'

'Well, I didn't intend carrying you on my back,' he remarked rather dryly, and she chuckled.

'But you're not going in my direction,' she exclaimed.

'No, but I'm quite prepared to do so. My car is just

parked along here. If you'd like a lift, that is.'

'Gosh, would I?' she cried in relief. 'Please.'

'Good.' He put a hand beneath her elbow and guided her swiftly along the busy street. She was intensely conscious of the nearness of him and of how attractive he looked in a dark blue suit and dark overcoat. The collar of his overcoat was turned up and she found him quite fascinating.

The car turned out to be a Rolls, while a uniformed chauffeur was seated behind the steering wheel. He sprang out at Adam's approach and said:

'Are you ready to go already, sir?'

'I am, Jules,' replied Caroline's companion smoothly. 'However, I intend to drive myself. You can go along to the office and explain that I've been called away and will be rather late.'

'Yes, sir.' The chauffeur saluted smartly. If he was at all surprised at this turn of events he did not show it and although the sight of Caroline in her rather shabby duffel coat could not have been a usual one his face remained impassive. After he had gone Caroline looked curiously at her companion. Who on earth could he be, to run a Rolls and a chauffeur? He must only be a director, she decided nervously, and bit hard at her lip.

Adam smiled at her obvious discomfiture. 'Don't look so perturbed,' he remarked lazily. 'The car belongs to me, I can assure you.'

Caroline flushed. 'I don't doubt that,' she replied, sighing and allowed him to assist her into the seat beside the driver. After closing her door firmly, he walked round the bonnet and slid in beside her. He looked perfectly at ease and she thought rather wistfully that he fitted the car. Both were well groomed and immaculate.

'And now,' he said, before she had any time to ask questions, 'where am I to take you?'

Caroline told him her address and wondered whether when they arrived he would expect to be invited in. She hoped not. The old building was hardly the sort of background she would have chosen.

Their route through some unknown side streets brought them to Gloucester Court in a very short time. As they had avoided the main roads the traffic had been much lighter and although Caroline was sure she would have got lost in the fog, it was obvious that this man knew London very well. The big car looked out of place in the small court and Caroline hoped Amanda was not looking out of the window. They had spoken little on the journey and when the car halted Caroline made to get out as quickly as she could.

'Just a moment,' he muttered easily. 'How long will you be?'

Caroline's eyes widened. 'Not long,' she exclaimed guardedly.

'Then I'll wait,' he said surprisingly, and took out a case of cigars.

Caroline was astounded, but with a hasty 'Thank you' she sprang out, carefully closed the door and ran inside the building.

The flat was on the first floor and soon she was unlocking the door and going in. A glance at her watch told her it was barely twelve-forty-five. Only a quarter of her hour had gone already.

Amanda was still in bed, breathing nasally. 'Is that you, Caroline?' she called feebly.

'Who were you expecting?' replied Caroline cheerfully. 'Now then, how do you feel?' She came to the bedroom door.

'I'm bearing up,' answered Amanda with a forced smile. 'You're nice and early. Could I have some soup, do you think? I feel quite hungry now.'

'Of course,' said Caroline, pulling off her mitts. 'That's a good sign.' She hurried into the kitchen and filled the kettle before opening the tin of beef broth.

When the kettle had boiled she refilled Amanda's hot water bottle again and made some more tea. She put ten pence in the electric meter, ensuring that the fire would remain on, and put the soup in a saucepan to heat up.

'Did you get into trouble this morning?' asked Amanda thickly, as Caroline set a tray of steaming soup, toast, and tea in front of her.

'Well, I'm still on the payroll,' replied Caroline, evading the question. She didn't want Amanda worrying about her and as for telling her about accepting a lift from a stranger! Well! She just couldn't do it. Amanda would think she was the village idiot; after all, she knew nothing about him at all.

After making Amanda comfortable, she put on her mitts again.

'I must go,' she said quickly. 'I don't want to be late again.'

Amanda's eyes widened. 'But, Caroline, it's only one o'clock and you've had nothing yourself.'

'Oh, I'm not hungry,' lied Caroline blithely, aware of feeling particularly empty. 'Anyway, I can get a sandwich from the canteen when I get back.'

'Oh, all right, pet. Thanks for everything, and mind

how you go. Let's hope I'm feeling better by tonight. I have a date with Ron.'

Ron Cartwright was her current boy-friend. A cub-reporter for the *Daily Southerner* who imagined himself the editor, was Caroline's private opinion.

'Well, you won't be going out,' stated Caroline indignantly. 'It's absolutely freezing out there, and it's so damp and foggy.'

Amanda shivered and sipped her soup appreciatively. 'All right, all right, it was only a thought.'

'Well, forget it,' ordered Caroline with a smile. 'I must go now.' She walked to the door. 'See you about five-thirty, I expect.'

'Okay, don't get lost.'

Caroline ran down the stairs again and out into the street. The cold atmosphere was numbing and feeling very nervous she approached the car. It had been turned in her absence and as she neared it the man pushed open the door from inside. She slid in beside him, into a world of luxurious comfort, warm air and the delicious scent of Havana tobacco.

'Good,' he said as she slammed the door. 'Do I take it you have executed your business?'

'Yes, sir,' Caroline was subdued.

'Sir?' He frowned. 'Why are you calling me that?'

Caroline shrugged. 'Well, you must be somebody important with a car like this,' she replied carefully. 'I don't know who you are, and if you don't mind my saying so, you don't seem awfully keen to tell me. Are you married and afraid your wife finds out? Oh, I hope that doesn't sound rude.'

He smiled slightly. 'I am not married,' he stated

firmly, 'and you can call me Adam. Does that satisfy you?'

Caroline flushed scarlet. 'Yes, sir. . .I mean Adam,' she answered, feeling rather foolish.

He started the car and they moved away from the kerb. However, once they had joined the main stream of traffic he took the opposite turning to the proper one and Caroline realised they were not going in the direction of the Steinbeck Building.

'Wh. . .where are you taking me?' she enquired, trying to keep her voice calm when suddenly it felt very shaky.

'To a roadhouse I know near Kingston,' he replied easily. 'I gather you haven't eaten yet, so over a meal you can tell me all your troubles.'

Caroline gasped. 'But I'm due at the office in twenty minutes,' she exclaimed. 'Oh, please, take me back.'

'Don't worry,' he murmured, quite amused at her expression. 'I'll speak to Miss Morgan myself. Relax.'

Caroline's tensed body suddenly went weak. What could she do now? She had been stupid and she was now paying the penalty. He could do what he liked with her! Take her where he liked, for that matter! It was her own fault for trusting him. She looked desperately out of the window and wondered whether, if she shouted for help, anyone would take any notice. Driving in a car like this the odds were decidedly against it.

She was most astonished therefore, when a short while later, the powerful car turned between the wrought iron gates of a driveway and drew up outside the imposing façade of a country house with 'The Copper Kettle' printed on a sign which hung over the doorway.

Adam slid out and walked round the bonnet to assist
Caroline to alight. She forestalled him, however, and
with a smile he slammed her door and locked it.

'Did you think I was kidnapping you?' he asked in
her ear, as he drew her through the entrance and into
the wide hallway.

'That thought had crossed my mind,' she admitted
with a smile, which she suddenly couldn't control.

At their entrance a waiter appeared immediately and
greeted them. 'Your usual table, Mr Steinbeck?' he
asked politely, his sophisticated eyes taking in the blue
duffel coat that Caroline was wearing and finding it
sadly lacking.

'Yes, thank you, André,' replied Adam, and urged
Caroline forward. But Caroline had been arrested by
the man's words.

'Steinbeck,' she whispered in an awed voice.
'Oh, glory!'

The restaurant was quite full, but a table near the
window was awaiting them. André saw them comfort-
ably seated and then produced the menu with a
flourish. All the diners looked with surprise at
Caroline. The women were all wearing expensive furs;
minks and sables; and the men were as immaculately
groomed as Caroline's companion.

Quite a number of people had greeted Adam, and
Caroline, now aware of his identity, felt awkward and
out of place. She wished that he had not turned out to
be so important a person. Had he been just an ordinary
person like herself he might have seriously become
interested in her, but now that she knew who he was
she was convinced that any interest he had in her must
be simply curiosity. She ought to have realised the day

she met him in the lift, by the impeccable cut of his clothes, that he was no ordinary office worker. It was fantastic to consider the difference in their positions and she sighed dejectedly.

Adam asked her if she had any preference regarding the food, but she shook her head and was glad when he said he would choose for her. What did she know about menus that were large enough to cover the table?

After he had ordered the meal the wine waiter appeared and there followed another discussion about the choice of wines. As an apéritif he ordered Martinis, and Caroline found herself with a glass in her hand and a cigarette between her fingers.

Looking about her, Caroline was extremely conscious of the limitations of her red pinafore dress and white jumper and was convinced she must be the topic of conversation of all these elegantly fashionable women. They must be wondering why such a man as Adam Steinbeck was giving her lunch when he was obviously much more accustomed to dining with the élite of society.

Her eyes returned to Adam as he smoked his cigarette and she saw wonderingly that his eyelashes were extremely long and thick. Combined with his dark skin, strong face and fathomless eyes, he was quite the most attractive man Caroline had ever seen. He had a kind of animal magnetism against which she felt herself to be completely defenceless.

Suddenly his eyes turned on her and caught her staring at him and she hastily drew on her cigarette and took a sip of her Martini. She choked in the process and had the ignominy of spluttering and coughing

arousing the amused attention of the whole of the restaurant.

Adam, however, was not perturbed and said softly:

'I suppose you ought not to be drinking that,
ought you?'

Caroline flushed anew. 'I'm almost eighteen,' she
exclaimed, feeling embarrassed.

'Almost, but not quite,' he remarked slowly. 'However, in this instance, no one but ourselves is aware
of the facts, so there need be no disgrace.'

Caroline, sure he was amusing himself by teasing
her, put down her drink before she made any more
mistakes.

'Why didn't you tell me immediately you were
Adam Steinbeck?' she said suddenly.

He shrugged. 'It was a new experience to be treated
like a fellow employee. I quite enjoyed it.'

She sighed. 'I never know when you're serious,' she
said, looking very young and vulnerable.

'Don't you?' he smiled. 'Perhaps that's just as well,'
he said enigmatically.

The meal was the most delicious Caroline had ever
tasted. A clear consommé was followed by fresh sal-
mon, then Aylesbury duckling and green peas and
finally a strawberry mousse.

'Strawberries in December!' she exclaimed in
delight, and Adam smiled rather indulgently, like an
uncle who was taking out his favourite niece for a
special treat.

When they were having cigarettes with coffee made
with fresh cream, she sighed contentedly.

'I gather you enjoyed it,' he remarked, dropping the
ash from his cigarette into the ashtray.

'Oh, I did,' she exclaimed. 'It was fabulous! I've never had such a meal.' She flushed. 'I must seem very stupid.'

'No, just very young,' he replied softly. 'Now, tell me about this morning.'

'Oh, my being late, you mean,' she said with a grimace. 'Amanda has got 'flu and I had to make sure she was comfortable before I left. I didn't know she was ill until I got up, you see, so consequently I was late. The fog delayed me too and Miss Morgan was positively breathing fire when I got in. Mind you, it was a quarter to ten, so I guess she was right in a way. Although she wouldn't let me explain and reported me to Mr Donnelly. I had to go and see him at eleven and although he was angry I think he understood. Miss Morgan rather ravages him, you know, and the poor man doesn't know what to do for the best.'

'Really?' Adam sounded intrigued, and suddenly Caroline realised just who she was talking to. With a hasty frown she exclaimed:

'You wouldn't cause any trouble about this, would you? I don't wan't to get anyone into trouble.'

He smiled. 'Don't worry. I'll treat what you've told me as confidential, although I think Miss Morgan needs taking down a peg or two.' He laughed softly. 'So Donnelly decided to keep you on, did he?'

'Yes. But I mustn't be late again, because if I am, I'll be dismissed.' She glanced at her watch. 'That's a joke, do you realise it's a quarter to three?'

He relaxed lazily, studying her flushed face. 'I've told you, don't worry. Today you certainly will not get fired. I personally vouch for that.'

Caroline smiled. 'Honestly, this is all like some

crazy dream,' she exclaimed. 'I still can't believe it's true. Even though I know I'm sitting here, it seems too fantastic.'

He smiled in return. 'But you have enjoyed it?' he asked interestedly.

She sighed. 'How could I do anything else?' she exclaimed. 'It's been marvellous!'

'Good, I'm glad.' He stubbed out his cigarette. 'Are you ready to go?'

A few minutes later they were back in the Rolls and heading towards the city. Caroline felt unusually depressed. It had all been so unexpected and exciting and now it was all over. The skyscraper structure of the Steinbeck Building was soon in sight and Adam parked the car in its earlier position which was apparently reserved for him.

As soon as the car had stopped, Caroline turned towards him impulsively. 'I can't thank you enough,' she said, sighing. 'I've really had a fabulous lunch and I hope I haven't been too much of a liability.'

He grinned, and rested his arms on the steering wheel. 'Not at all,' he said easily. 'Tell me, would you like to have dinner with me one evening?'

Caroline's cheeks grew scarlet. 'Me?' she exclaimed. 'Why, I. . .are you sure you want to take me?'

He smiled lazily. 'Why else would I ask you? How about tomorrow?'

Caroline clasped her hands. Suddenly the day was much brighter. 'Oh, I'd adore it,' she cried.

'Good. I'll pick you up outside your apartment at seven. Is that too early?'

'No, I can manage that,' she answered eagerly. 'I'd better go now.'

'Hold on,' he exclaimed, sliding out from behind the wheel. 'I, too, am going into the building. And I too, am very late.'

'But you won't want to be seen with me,' she protested, and was surprised at the look of annoyance that crossed his face.

'Do you personally object?' he queried quietly.

'Of course not,' she denied swiftly.

'Then don't say that again,' he said curtly, and taking her arm firmly he led her towards the entrance.

It was three-fifteen and Caroline's legs felt like jelly. Her consternation must have shown in her face, because he said:

'Relax, I've told you, you'll be all right.'

She looked up at him and suddenly felt assured. The touch of his fingers on her elbow, the nearness of his strong, powerful body all reassured her and she knew she would always feel safe and secure with him.

They entered the impressive reception hall of the Steinbeck Building and were immediately the cynosure of all eyes. The intimacy of their relationship seemed suddenly blatant for all to see and self-consciously Caroline released herself from his hold.

The hall staff were quite obviously astounded and once they were inside the lift Adam turned thoughtfully to her.

'You were embarrassed,' he said softly. 'Why?'

Caroline shrugged, turning pink. 'I was thinking of you,' she said.

'What about me? That I was very much older than you?' He sounded amused.

'No,' denied Caroline hotly. 'It's just that those porters are such dreadful gossips and the whole building will know we came in together by tea-time.'

'And so?' he prompted. He was leaning against the wall of the lift. It had stopped at the third floor, but he made no attempt to open the gates.

'Well, don't you care?' she asked, aware of a breathlessness about her.

'Should I?' he asked, shrugging his shoulders carelessly. 'What I do is my own affair, surely. Are you sure it isn't yourself who feels upset?'

'Not at all,' exclaimed Caroline. 'Honestly, I quite enjoyed the feeling of being important for once.'

'Then you do still want to have dinner with me, tomorrow?'

Caroline moved her shoulders in a helpless gesture. 'Of course. I'm looking forward to it.'

'Good.' Straightening up, he opened the gates and allowed her to pass through. 'Then I'll see you tomorrow as arranged.' He smiled. 'I trust you have no trouble with Miss Morgan.'

He pressed the button for his floor and the lift went on up. Sighing, Caroline walked along to the typing pool. It was three-thirty.

It really was amazing, thought Caroline later that same afternoon, how very charming Miss Morgan could be when it suited her. It had been obvious from the moment that Caroline entered the large office which reverberated with the sound of a score of machines that Vera Morgan had been forewarned of her delayed return from lunch. Caroline was asked politely whether she had enjoyed herself and then advised that the other girls would help her if she had not got time to finish her work herself.

But Caroline did not think it fair to delegate her work to the others who had plenty to do themselves, so she worked steadily all the rest of the afternoon, and by five o'clock she was almost up to date. Sufficiently so to inform Miss Morgan that she could manage on her own in the morning.

Miss Morgan was aware of an unwilling admiration for Caroline, upon hearing this. Many girls in her position, although what that position was she was not quite sure, would have taken advantage of the situation and purposely sat back and allowed their work to be done by the others. As it was, Caroline had contrived to do all her work herself and Miss Morgan was quite pleasantly surprised.

When Caroline arrived home she found Amanda up and dressed, but she looked very pale and wan.

'You should have stayed in bed,' exclaimed Caroline, sitting down to sausage and eggs prepared by Amanda. Actually, Caroline did not feel very hungry after her enormous lunch, but she made a show of enjoying the meal so as not to hurt Amanda's feelings.

'Oh, well,' replied Amanda, having only one sausage herself and a slice of toast, 'with Ron arriving at six-thirty I had to do something.'

Caroline snorted in disapproval. 'You're not going out,' she stated flatly, and Amanda had to laugh.

'All right, don't fly off the handle,' she answered, sighing. 'I only wanted to look reasonably fit, that's all. As it is I feel as though I'm dying on my feet.'

Caroline shook her head. As if she couldn't have put Ron Cartwright off until another evening! She finished her tea and cleared away the dishes. While she washed up, Amanda re-did her face, heavily, disguising as best she could the hollows beneath her eyes and the greyish pallor of her skin. She still looked very drawn when Caroline came back in and she was about to tell her to get herself back to bed when the doorbell rang.

Caroline answered it and let in Ron Cartwright. As usual he looked cheekily pleased with himself, but he stopped dead at the sight of Amanda.

'Blimey!' he exclaimed, taking a step back. 'Marley's ghost!'

Amanda looked gloomily at Caroline. 'Ha. . .ha,' she said, with a forced smile.

'Hey, really, doll,' went on Ron, 'you do look a sketch. What's wrong?'

'She's got flu,' said Caroline. 'I'm sure you don't want to catch it, do you?' this last very pointedly.

Ron shrugged. 'Well, there's a thing,' he commented, flinging himself on to the couch. 'I guess the flicks is out for us, then.'

Caroline winced at his language and looked at Amanda with raised eyebrows. Amanda took the hint.

'Yes. I'm going back to bed.'

'I see,' Ron turned his gaze speculatively on Caroline. 'How about you and me taking in a show?' he asked brightly.

Amanda gasped. 'Don't mind me!' she snorted, and flounced into the bedroom slamming the door.

'What's bitten her?' asked Ron blandly. 'Well, Caroline? What about it?'

'You must be joking,' said Caroline, a look of distaste on her face.

Ron was undaunted. 'You know I always fancied a date with you,' he said, standing up. He tried to grasp her wrist playfully, but she twisted away from him.

'Don't you dare to touch me!' she exclaimed furiously. 'You can leave just as soon as you like, Mr Cartwright!'

Ron shrugged, still confidently unabashed. 'Okay, doll. I'm going. Nobody can say that Ron Cartwright forces his attentions where they're not wanted. It's not necessary, chum. I can date a dozen like you just as easily as that.' He snapped his fingers in her face.

'Then go and find one,' retorted Caroline wearily. 'Really, you overgrown approved-schoolboys appal me!'

That caught him on a sore spot, for he flung her a baleful glance before sauntering out.

Caroline closed the door after him and went into the bedroom to find Amanda. She was back in bed and surprisingly was smiling.

'I heard,' she said before Caroline could speak. 'I guess we've seen the last of him.'

'Well, honestly,' exclaimed Caroline ruefully, 'how you could become involved with anyone like him amazes me. He's so boring.'

Amanda shrugged. 'Beggars can't be choosers,' she replied, sighing. 'You may find out one day. Girls like you and me just don't meet up with the cream of the male population.'

Caroline flushed scarlet. She had not told Amanda about her second meeting with Adam Steinbeck or their subsequent lunch together. She realised with a sense of shock that comparing Ron Cartwright with

Adam was like comparing tomato juice with champagne.

Amanda had noticed her heightened colour, however, and said perceptively: 'Have you seen that dreamboat from the lift again, by any chance?'

Caroline moved restlessly, now she had no choice but to tell Amanda.

'As a matter of fact,' she said casually, 'I saw him at lunch time.'

'Oh, really?' Amanda's eyes were huge. 'How?'

'Well, actually, I bumped into him outside the offices and when I told him I was rushing home he offered me a lift in his car.'

Amanda gasped. 'Caroline Sinclair,' she exclaimed accusingly. 'You weren't going to tell me this, were you?'

'Of course,' retorted Caroline. 'I've not had the chance before. Anyway, he brought me home. That's how I was so early.'

'Indeed. Weren't you being rather reckless? After all, you don't know the man. Did you find out his name?'

Caroline hesitated. 'Well, yes. He's Adam Steinbeck.' It came out with a rush and Amanda's face was a picture, registering astonishment, incredulity and finally disbelief with lightning rapidity.

'Are you serious?' she gasped, a hand to her cheek. '*The* Adam Steinbeck?'

Caroline sighed, feeling slightly overawed herself. 'Yes. It was a surprise to me too.'

'Surprise?' cried Amanda. 'It's nothing short of a miracle. No wonder poor old Ron got the cold shoulder. You're playing for higher stakes.'

Caroline frowned. 'It's not like that at all,' she said irritably.

Amanda shook her head, bewildered. 'And you were serious that day when you said you didn't know who he was?'

'Of course. Good heavens, Amanda, I've only been there three weeks. How could I possibly recognise him? Anyway, I didn't.'

'It really is fantastic. And you say he's an attractive man?'

'He's fabulous,' exclaimed Caroline, hugging herself suddenly. 'By the way, he took me to lunch at a roadhouse called the Copper Kettle.'

If it had been possible for Amanda to look even more shocked she would have done so.'

'He's a very nice person,' went on Caroline. 'He made me feel at ease. I didn't get back to work until three-thirty and Miss Morgan was as nice as pie.' She smiled. 'Yes, he's very nice indeed.'

Amanda looked wryly at her. 'Millionaires couldn't be anything else in my book,' she said, sighing. 'Boy, do you have all the luck!'

'His money doesn't particularly appeal to me,' replied Caroline lazily, flinging herself on the foot of her bed. 'I'd probably be better pleased if he was just a two-thousand-a-year clerk. At least he might seriously be interested in me then. As it is. . .'

'Now, hold on,' exclaimed Amanda sitting up. 'Lunch is all right, dinner maybe, but as for getting seriously involved with a man of his age, well, you must be joking!'

Caroline flushed. 'Don't say that,' she said tensely.

Amanda frowned. 'Why not? Someone's got to.

Think, Caroline! He probably eats girls like you for breakfast. Men like Steinbeck can have their pick of any woman, and I mean any woman. Be your age. Besides, he's probably married with half a dozen kids.'

Caroline rolled on to her suddenly churning stomach.

'He said he wasn't married,' she muttered quietly. 'I can easily find out if he's lying, so why should he lie?'

Amanda shrugged. 'Okay, he's not married. That doesn't make him any younger.'

Caroline clenched her teeth. Amanda was probably right in everything she said, but she still wanted to see him again. She had to see him again! She had never heard anything derogatory spoken about him at the office, but that was no guarantee; money could close a lot of mouths.

'Well, anyway,' she said defiantly, 'I'm having dinner with him tomorrow night.'

Amanda spread her hands, palms upwards. 'I can't stop you. I can only say that the Steinbeck Building must have been up about fifteen years and he's been there probably as the head for most of that time.'

Caroline sighed. 'I expect he's in his thirties,' she said casually.

'Late thirties,' corrected Amanda grimly. 'Hell, you're really hooked aren't you? I'm sorry, kid, but you shouldn't take people at their face value.'

Caroline shrugged. 'You're a great one to talk. What about you and that creature who called this evening?'

Amanda frowned. 'At least he's in my age and income group,' she retorted, and Caroline got up off her bed and walked moodily into the living-room.

No matter what Amanda said, she was going.

CHAPTER TWO

THE following morning the office was buzzing with the news that Caroline Sinclair, the new girl in the typing pool, had been seen entering the building with Adam Steinbeck himself. It was also rumoured that they had had lunch together.

Caroline herself had got up earlier to look after Amanda before leaving home and had arrived on time. Ruth could hardly wait to speak to her.

'Is it true?' she gasped. 'Was that why you were so late back yesterday? You had no time to tell me, being so busy when you got back.'

'Yes,' admitted Caroline reluctantly. 'And please, before you start too, I don't want a lecture.'

Ruth looked surprised at Caroline's tone of voice. 'Pardon me for asking,' she said in a hurt voice. 'Seriously though, Caroline, before you bite my head off, he is about forty, you know.'

Caroline closed her eyes for a moment. 'Now, Ruth. . .' she began.

'Oh, I know, he's a dish,' interrupted Ruth quickly, 'I've seen him in the distance myself. I expect dozens of women adore him, but really, you don't honestly believe he's interesting himself in you for any other reason than the obvious one.'

'Which is?' said Caroline irritably.

'Why, sex, of course,' replied Ruth, flushing.

Caroline sighed. 'I honestly don't know why you

and Amanda think you know Adam Steinbeck better than me. Amanda wouldn't know him if she saw him and you've just admitted you've only seen him from a distance. You both seem to think he's some sort of sex-maniac or something.'

Ruth shrugged. 'We're only thinking of you,' she returned coolly. 'Have you considered what would happen if you get more than friendly? He's not some boy who expects a goodnight kiss in a doorway. He was married, he'll expect rather more.'

'Married!' exclaimed Caroline. 'What happened to his wife?'

'She died of leukaemia about eight years ago. One of the older girls told me about it ages ago.'

'I see,' Caroline could not help but feel relieved. At least he had not been lying to her. 'Has he any family, then?'

'He has a son, he's at Radbury University, I believe. Good heavens, Caroline, his son is older than you are.'

Caroline clenched her fists. 'Truthfully, Ruth, would you think he was too old for you, if you were in my place?'

Ruth was silent. In her heart of hearts she knew that Caroline had her cornered. A man like Steinbeck could not be ignored even without his wealth and position. And to have him invite you to lunch must be very exciting.

'All right,' she agreed at last. 'In your position I'd probably do the same. But I wouldn't take him seriously, Caroline. Things like that just don't happen outside of story books. Anyway, how on earth did you meet him?'

'You remember the man in the lift?' asked Caroline quietly.

'You don't mean that was Steinbeck?'

Caroline nodded.

'My gosh!' Ruth was astounded. 'Do you mean to say he asked you out that day and you didn't tell me?'

'No, I bumped into him yesterday lunch time when I was rushing home to see Amanda. He offered me a lift and I accepted. Then he asked me to lunch.'

Ruth shrugged helplessly. 'Well, well, well.' She sighed. 'But do be careful, Caroline. I really mean it.'

'All right.' Caroline turned away to her machine. She did not intend mentioning her dinner date. She had heard quite enough comments about him for the time being.

The morning dragged by. She did not have to go home at lunch as Amanda was feeling a lot better after her day in bed and had said she could get herself something to eat.

As she worked, Caroline wondered what on earth she was going to wear that evening. She had only one evening dress, which she had worn last at a party given by the secretarial college where she had taken the course. It was dated already and being of pink cotton, chosen by Aunt Agnes, it made her look very young and schoolgirlish.

She eventually decided she would have to have a new dress. She called at the Post Office during her lunch hour and drew out twenty pounds of her savings. She knew she was being ridiculously extravagant, but she wanted Adam to be proud of her.

After work, in a small dress shop near the office building, she found exactly what she wanted. It was jade green, of see-through lace, and Caroline felt quite daring. The colour matched her eyes and she looked years older than her seventeen years. She felt very satisfied. Now she could hold her own with any of those sleek, society women.

Amanda was horrified when she found Caroline had wasted so much money; and wasted was the word she used.

'You must be mad!' she exclaimed angrily. 'Don't you realise that if you were to go out regularly with a man like him you would need loads of new clothes? I know you've only got fifty pounds in the Post Office, because you told me so.'

Caroline swung round furiously. 'Really, Amanda, it's my money, after all!'

'You want your head examining,' retorted Amanda fiercely.

'Just leave me alone,' muttered Caroline. 'I'll tread my own path to destruction, if you don't mind.'

Amanda was silent for a moment and then she said:

'I'm sorry if I sound interfering. It's simply that you can't afford to spend all that money on one outfit.' She sighed. 'Oh, well, if you really intend going through with it, do you want to borrow my cape?'

Caroline flushed and then looked ashamed. 'Please, Amanda.' She sighed. 'Oh, I'm sorry if I was rude, really I am, but I can take care of myself.'

Amanda shrugged. 'All right. I won't say another word. What time is he arriving?'

Caroline told her and then rushed away to take a bath before someone else collared the bathroom. She was ready as the clock from the nearby church steeple struck seven o'clock. She looked beautiful in the green dress. Amanda was aware that she looked much older tonight, but refrained from saying so in case she caused another row.

It was she who first saw the Rolls turn into the cul-de-sac and turning come to halt by the door below.

'I guess this is him,' she said slowly, while Caroline felt her stomach palpitate alarmingly.

'I'll go down,' she said, opening the door.

'Be good,' remarked Amanda with a wry smile. Then more seriously, 'And be careful.'

Caroline nodded, and then closing the door she descended the stairs.

When she reached the street she found Adam leaning against the bonnet of the car, smoking a cigarette. Tonight he was wearing a charcoal grey suit and a dark grey gabardine overcoat. He looked bigger than ever as he straightened at her approach.

'Hello,' she murmured, and his eyes narrowed rather mockingly before he too smiled at her.

'Good evening,' he answered suavely, and opened the car door for her to slide in.

When he was seated beside her he gave her an appraising look. 'You look quite beautiful, my dear,' he said rather sardonically. 'And very sophisticated too. Are you?'

Not liking his tone, Caroline shivered suddenly. 'I. . .I don't think I quite understand you,' she replied, trying to see his face in the semi-darkness.

He sounded amused and said: 'Forget it.'

The car was as smooth and luxurious as Caroline remembered and she relaxed slightly in her seat.

'I've booked a table at the Mozambo for eight

o'clock,' he remarked as the car joined the busier traffic of the King's Road. The Mozambo was a newly-opened night-club and Caroline knew she ought not to go anywhere like that as she was not yet eighteen.

Adam glanced at her when she did not reply. 'What's wrong?' he asked blandly. 'Don't you like the idea? I'm sure it's just the place for an outfit like that.'

'It's not that I don't want to go,' she answered uncomfortably. 'But as I'm not eighteen until March. . .'

'Ah, I had forgotten,' he said slowly, although she had the feeling he had not forgotten at all. 'Then we will go somewhere more innocuous.'

Caroline felt dreadfully young and gauche. 'Oh, really,' she murmured. 'I feel rather ridiculous.'

'Why? You can't help your age. Besides, night-clubs are not particularly my metier.'

Caroline sighed, still feeling uncomfortable. 'Then where are we going?'

Adam looked thoughtful. 'I think perhaps we will have dinner at the Caprice and then I'll get tickets for a show. Is there any particular show you would care to see?'

'I really don't mind,' exclaimed Caroline, half relieved. 'Are you sure I'm not spoiling your evening?'

He smiled wryly. 'You couldn't do that,' he replied smoothly.

The Caprice was as exciting as she had imagined. She recognised some famous celebrities as they were shown to their table and she felt amazed at the ease with which Adam dealt with the waiters. Although the restaurant was extremely busy he had had no difficulty in acquiring a table, and it was obvious he was both liked and respected.

Before ordering the meal Adam ordered himself a whisky, but Caroline was given a lime and lemon, much to her chagrin. She accepted the cigarette he offered her and said: 'Do you think it's safe for me to have this?' in a rather dry tone.

Adam smiled, studying the menu with an experienced eye. 'Have you decided what you want to eat?' he asked, ignoring her remark.

'No. I'll leave it to you. I'm afraid I'm not used to dining in places like this.' She sounded rather wistful and for a moment Adam's rather sardonic expression relaxed. Then drawing deeply on his cigarette he returned to his contemplation of the menu.

Once the meal was ordered, Adam transferred his attention to his companion.

'I'm glad you decided to come,' he said easily.

'Did you think I might not?' she asked, surprised.

'Well, I must admit I had my doubts,' he replied lazily. 'I imagine all your friends have been warning you against getting mixed up with a man like me?'

'How did you ..?' she began, and then stopped, flushing.

'So I was right,' he murmured. 'And what was your reason for not taking their advice?'

'I told them I was quite capable of taking care of myself,' she replied, refusing to meet his eyes.

'I see.' He nodded. 'And do you really believe that?'

Caroline flushed deeper. 'Well, of course,' she exclaimed quickly. 'If I didn't I shouldn't have come.'

'Worthy sentiments,' he remarked dryly, but when she did look up at him his eyes were mocking.

His eyes strayed across the revealing lace of her dress, almost insolently, and Caroline had the urge to cover herself. She wished she had never bought this particular dress, but something more in keeping with her age and personality.

When his eyes returned to hers she felt she was blushing all over and he smiled mockingly. 'Not quite so sophisticated?' he enquired sardonically, and Caroline felt her nerves jumping. Suddenly the advice she had been given by Amanda and Ruth became reasonable.

The meal, when it was served, was delicious, but Caroline ate very little. During the intervals between the numerous courses Adam spoke casually about his journeys abroad and for a while Caroline's tension relaxed and she enjoyed listening to him. He was a fascinating raconteur and his stories were often amusing and edifying.

Afterwards, Caroline decided on a show she would like to see and the evening became less of a strain. The show was a light musical comedy and it helped to relieve Caroline's uncertainty. Adam was a good companion when he was not mocking her and she gradually relaxed completely.

When the show was over they walked back to where the car was awaiting them and got inside swiftly out of the cold night air. Adam started the engine and drove out into the main stream of traffic with expert technique. Caroline was so fascinated by his lean hands on the wheel that at first she did not realise they were not heading in the direction of the flat. When she did realise it they were already turning into a quiet mews in Mayfair. Caroline clasped her handbag tightly.

Where on earth was he taking her? She was so shocked that she sat in speechless amazement when he stopped the car below a low doorway of what seemed to be a mews cottage. The mews was completely private, lit by one lamp, and only this one dwelling opened on to it. All the newspaper stories she had read of girls getting attacked and murdered flooded into her terrified mind as she sat there while Adam slid out and walked round the bonnet to her side.

When he opened her door, the automatic light in the car illuminated her frightened face and he sighed and said:

'Don't look like that. I'm not going to harm you. Come on. Out!'

Mutely, shivering slightly, Caroline slid out. She felt stiff and awkward and somehow fatalistic. Whatever was going to happen would happen whatever she did.

With another half-disgusted look at her, Adam opened the door and switched on the light inside. Then he drew back to allow her to precede him inside. When they were both standing in the low hallway he closed the door. Caroline was conscious of a ruby red carpet beneath her feet which spread up the wide shallow staircase. The walls were darkly panelled and the lighting was concealed, casting a warm glow about them.

Adam passed her and walked down the hall, removing his overcoat as he went.

'You can leave your wrap here,' he said coolly, and Caroline slipped off her coat and laid it on an exquisitely-carved polished chest which stood at one end of the hall. On the chest was a vase of chrysanthemums whose curly yellow petals made a splash of colour against the dark woodwork. It really was the most attractive hall Caroline had ever seen and curiosity getting the better of her she followed Adam down the hall and through a doorway. She found herself in yet another exquisitely decorated room. This was a low lounge with a pseudo-log fire burning in a wide fireplace of white brick. The carpet here changed to sapphire blue and low couches of white velvet invited the visitor. A carved cocktail cabinet stood beneath windows which were now hidden by blue velvet curtains and the whole effect was one of luxurious relaxation. Adam stood on the hearth regarding her as she hesitated just within the doorway.

'Well?' he asked expectantly, 'do you like it?'

Caroline raised her shoulders helplessly. Getting her voice back, she murmured, 'You know it's quite fabulous.' She sighed. 'My opinion can be of no interest to you.'

Adam shrugged and then crossed to the cocktail cabinet. 'Will you have a drink?'

Immediately her earlier fears returned and Adam, looking at her, must have sensed this, for he said:

'Don't bother to refuse. I think a small brandy might restore your confidence.'

Caroline shrugged and took the glass when he handed it to her. Amusement playing over his handsome face, he deliberately crossed to the double white doors and closed them firmly. Then turning once more to Caroline he indicated a low couch. 'Won't you sit down?'

Caroline subsided quickly, glad to be off her rather shaky legs. To her dismay, Adam seated himself beside her and lay back lazily resting his dark head against the white velvet. Caroline, glancing at him, was over-whelmingly aware of his physical attraction that reached out to her like a magnet and made her feel breathlessly weak.

'Now,' he said slowly, 'let's get one thing straight, shall we?'

Caroline frowned. 'What's that?' she asked nervously.

Adam stretched his legs luxuriously. 'Well,' he murmured, 'you are under a misapprehension regarding both yourself and me.' He lit a cigarette slowly before continuing. 'When we first met you were very relaxed with me and I liked that. I know at first you didn't know who I was, but even after you did you were still relaxed...natural. Now, suddenly, after all this brainwashing by your so-called friends you're terrified of me. Why? What do you expect me to do? Attack you?'

Caroline flushed. She felt suddenly very stupid.

He frowned and went on: 'And tonight you arrive to meet me looking like nothing on earth! That dress would suit a woman of thirty. It's far too old for you. Sure I baited you about being sophisticated because I was so mad that you should think you have to dress like that to suit me. You've transformed yourself into just another female. I hadn't booked a table at the Mozambo at all. I just wondered how far that veneer of sophistication would take you. If you'd agreed to go to that night-club I would have put you over my knee. Now do you understand? I asked you out because you were what you were...fresh, young, innocent if you like, but not because I wanted a dressed-up doll to take to dinner. God, don't you think I get sick of women flinging themselves at me, women who look just like you do tonight? That's not bigheadedness either. I guess money appeals to most women.'

He rose to his feet suddenly and crossed to the cocktail cabinet and poured himself another drink.

Caroline sipped her drink. She felt about six years old and about as many inches high. 'What now?' she murmured, her voice husky and near to tears. She had a pain in her inside that threatened to overwhelm her and she couldn't understand it.

He shrugged and replaced his glass beside the decanter. 'I guess we'll have to start again,' he replied with a lazy smile. Then seeing the tears in Caroline's eyes he exclaimed: 'Hey, did you think I just brought you here to lecture you and then never see you again?'

Caroline nodded and brushed a hand over her eyes. Relief flooded over her and with a piercing insight she realised why she had been so frightened; why she had not wanted it to end! She was in love with this man; loved him so completely that she knew she would never be the same again.

She forced herself to look at him without emotion when he flung himself beside her again and said:

'Now, tomorrow is Saturday. Would you like to drive into the country with me and come and see my house near Windsor? This place is just somewhere in town where I can stay or work if necessary. I have a housekeeper, but I believe she's away for the weekend. At any rate she didn't expect me this evening.'

'I'd adore to come,' exclaimed Caroline eagerly, smiling at him. 'Does this mean we're alone here at the moment?'

'Yes,' he murmured with a sigh. 'But don't get any

more ideas. I'm going to take you home right now.'
He rose to his feet and offered her a hand to get up.
Taking it, Caroline's stomach plunged. Far from wanting to leave she longed to cling to him, suddenly afraid
at the tumult of feelings he had aroused.

It did not take long to reach Gloucester Court and
Caroline slid reluctantly out of the warm intimacy of
the big car. Adam escorted her to the entrance of
the flats.

'I'll collect you from here at about three o'clock
tomorrow afternoon,' he said, smiling down at her.
'Just wear something casual.'

She laughed softly, looking up at him. 'Leopard-skin
tights and a backless sweater,' she teased him.

'God, no,' he muttered, turning away. 'Go on. I'll
see you tomorrow. Goodnight.'

Amanda was not asleep when Caroline entered the
bedroom and she had to relate the night's events. She
omitted the visit to his mews residence, however, but
although it was already eleven-thirty, Amanda seemed
satisfied that they had come straight home. Caroline
resolved not to discuss Adam with Amanda or Ruth
in future. Their knowledge was only based on hearsay;
Caroline felt she knew Adam much better than that.

Amanda returned to work on the Saturday morning,
for although it was half-day closing a lot of her work
was done after closing hours. This made things easier
for Caroline who decided to leave a note telling
Amanda where she had gone, thus evading any further
discussion of Adam's merits.

She washed her hair in the morning, scrambled an
egg for lunch and was ready by two-thirty. She had

dressed in Black Watch tartan trews and a bulky blue sweater and carried her duffel coat. With her silvery hair loose and wearing little make-up she looked young and wholesome.

She saw a low white continental car turn into the mews at a quarter to three and wondered idly whose car it was. She did not connect it with Adam until there was a knock at her door.

She hurried to open it, inwardly praying it wasn't Aunt Agnes, who sometimes took it into her head to visit Caroline on Saturday afternoons. However, when she opened the door and saw Adam she gasped and said:

'Why, Adam!' in a surprised tone. 'I've been watching for you, but I didn't see the car.'

He shrugged and walked past her into the room, looking about him with interest. 'Are you ready?' he asked. 'At least you look your age today.'

Caroline smiled. 'I'll take that as a compliment,' she answered lightly. 'But don't look round here. It's all so old and untidy, I'm afraid.'

Adam nodded critically. 'These old houses should all be demolished,' he said, noticing the damp patch under the windows which Amanda had unsuccessfully tried to hide with a leather print. 'A new block of flats would house twice as many people and be more hygienic.' He smiled at Caroline. 'Shall we go?'

Today he was dressed in dark slacks and a navy blue sweater over a blue shirt. He was wearing his sheepskin coat and looked big and handsome. Caroline inwardly hugged herself as they went down to the car. A whole afternoon and possibly evening too with him all to herself.

To her surprise, Adam crossed to the white car. It looked sleek and powerful and she felt excited as she got in.

'This is why I didn't see you,' she explained as he joined her in the automobile. 'I only looked for the Rolls.'

'Hm,' he murmured in reply. 'I decided the Rolls was in need of a check-up, so I brought this instead.'

'I like it,' exclaimed Caroline eagerly. 'It's more. . . well. . .'

'Intimate,' he suggested lazily, and she flushed.

'Casual,' she replied, then with a sigh of contentment she continued: 'Oh, I'm so glad you invited me to come with you today. By the way, how did you find our apartment?'

Adam started the car. 'Caro, honey, you work for me,' he answered, and Caroline smiled and nodded. No one else had ever abbreviated her name to 'Caro' and she adored it, just as she adored the way he said it.

The drive to his home was smooth and comfortable and very fast. They drove beyond Windsor to a village called Slayford and on the outskirts of the village they turned between the drive gates of a low, modern villa-bungalow. It was a massive place designed on Grecian lines with statuary in the forecourt and a fountain playing into a small pool. The drive swept round the fountain and Adam brought the car to a halt before double glass doors with a wrought iron grille covering the inside. Wide, shallow steps led up to these doors crossing a pillar-supported terrace.

'Gosh,' exclaimed Caroline, forestalling Adam as he would have helped her from the car, 'I never imagined anything like this. It's quite fabulous.'

'I'm glad you like it,' he replied, thrusting his hands deep into the pockets of his coat. 'I had it built five years ago to my own specifications.'

Drawing out his keys, he opened the doors and they stepped into a pile-carpeted hallway. Caroline's feet sank deep into the carpet and she stared about her in wonderment. If the mews cottage had been luxurious, this place was doubly so. The warmth of the central heating met you at your entrance while the air was kept fresh by a conditioning system.

The hall was wide and high and a crystal chandelier hung above them. A fan-shaped staircase lay ahead of them leading to the upper regions of the house and everywhere was carpeted in this heather-mixture coloured pile. The walls depicted hunting scenes in hand-painted murals, and Caroline felt sure she would never know which of the numerous doors opening off the hall opened into where.

Then a door at the far end of the hall opened and a middle-aged woman came hurrying through, a spaniel at her heels. The spaniel made a beeline for Adam, barking excitedly and wagging its short tail.

'Meet Mrs Jones and Nero,' said Adam, laughing at Caroline. 'Mrs Jones, this is Miss Sinclair.'

'How do you do, miss,' smiled the motherly little woman. 'And what a surprise this is,' she exclaimed, looking at Adam indulgently. 'But it's very glad we are to see you again, sir. Jones is chopping logs over at the woodshed just now, but he'll be back directly if you want to see him.'

'That's all right, Mrs Jones,' said Adam, removing his overcoat.

'The fire is lit in the lounge, just in case you wanted

it,' went on Mrs Jones. 'If you'd like to go in there I'll bring you some tea just as soon as the kettle boils.'

Mrs Jones was round and fat and jolly, and Caroline took an immediate liking to her. As for Nero, he was a bundle of mischief and pranced round them as they entered the lounge. A big log fire burned in the grate and the room looked cosily inviting. Here the carpet changed to moss green while the low couches and armchairs were upholstered in dark red brocade. The wide windows overlooked the rear of the house where green lawns stretched down to a large swimming pool which had been emptied for the winter. Beyond the pool were tennis courts, but Adam drew the rich curtains across the windows as it was already quite dark, and switched on a tall standard lamp, thus curtailing Caroline's gaze.

'This is the only room in the house where there is an open fire,' he remarked as she seated herself on one of the couches near the fire. 'It's simply that I enjoy seeing a real fire now and again.'

'Oh, so do I,' agreed Caroline, a sense of well-being stealing over her.

Adam came to sit beside her, and Caroline wondered whether he had any idea of the effect he had on her. She thought gloomily that he probably considered her simply as a rather nice child to whom he was giving a treat.

He stretched out his legs towards the blaze lazily and smiled at her.

'This is the life,' he remarked, lighting two cigarettes and handing her one. 'Away from big business, trusts, high finance, land speculation. . .' He groaned and closed his eyes.

Caroline smiled, looking intently at him. It was hard to conceive that on this man the livelihoods of several hundred employees rested. Just how many people depended upon his judgement? The Steinbeck Building housed a lot of different companies all owned by the Steinbeck Corporation and each one relied to a certain extent on Adam Steinbeck. He was the chairman of the board, he had the deciding vote if such a thing was necessary and he was responsible if there were any mistakes. She wished she had the courage to move closer to him and massage his temples. Aunt Agnes used to like her to do that; she said it soothed away all her tension.

Suddenly there was a tap at the door and Mrs Jones entered with a tray of tea, sandwiches and hot home-made scones.

Adam opened his eyes and sat up reluctantly. 'Thank you, Mrs Jones. Do you think we could have dinner at about seven-thirty?'

'Surely,' she replied with a twinkle in her eye. 'Now, you have a nice hot scone, and ring if you want more tea.'

'Bless you,' said Adam, and Mrs Jones chuckled as she went out.

Nero, who had settled himself in front of the fire also, now smelt food and Caroline allowed him to eat some of her sandwiches.

'You'll make him fat,' remarked Adam with a grin. 'He's been badly spoiled by the Joneses.'

Caroline shrugged. 'I know. . .but his eyes positively implore for more. He's very persuasive and very lovable.'

'Lucky Nero,' said Adam rather dryly, and drank his tea.

When they had finished with the tray, Caroline placed it on the table near the door.

'Ought I to take it through?' she offered anxiously. She wasn't used to having everything done for her in such a manner, pleasant though it might be.

'No,' he drawled lazily. 'Come and sit beside me and tell me all about yourself.'

Caroline's heart pounded as she seated herself beside him, intensely aware of his thigh only inches away from her own and of his head turned her way, eyes watching her, as he relaxed against the red brocade. The lighting from the standard lamp was not bright and Caroline hoped he was unaware of how much he disturbed her.

'There's not much to tell,' she murmured quietly, gazing into the fire. 'My parents died when I was very young. An aunt brought me up and then I moved in with Amanda six months ago.'

'Very exciting,' he remarked with a smile. 'No romance?'

The intimacy of this situation washed over her and she shook her head, not trusting herself to speak. How could she make light-hearted conversation about a subject so newly apparent?

Adam moved slightly, until his thigh was touching hers, and cupped her face with one hand, forcing her to look at him. His eyes scanned her features intently, and she was sure he must be able to hear the thudding of her heart. She trembled violently, and jerked her face away before he could read what must be in her eyes. She felt his fingers playing with her hair, touching the nape of her neck, disturbing her emotions, so that she was forced to look at him again. Then, slowly and deliberately, he leant forward, and placed his mouth against hers, exploring its softness expertly, until her lips parted involuntarily, and the kiss hardened and lengthened into something much more demanding. Caroline had never dreamed a man's mouth could arouse such sensations, and it was with a sense of loss she felt him release her and get up, with almost savage movements.

Caroline remained where she was, unknowingly provocative in her untried innocence.

Adam angrily kicked a log in the fire with his shoe, and stood staring down into the flames.

'Why don't you say something?' he muttered. 'Like, for instance, what about last night's lecture?'

Caroline sighed. 'Are you sorry you kissed me, Adam?' she asked softly.

Adam swung round. 'You know what I want to do!' he groaned violently. 'Me! The so-called platonic adviser of last night!' He frowned angrily. 'And I thought I could bring you here and take you back without incident.' He ran a hand over his hair. 'I must have been mad!'

Caroline shook her head. 'Stop torturing yourself, Adam,' she said quietly. 'It was my fault.'

Adam breathed swiftly. 'Caroline, don't make it any harder!'

Caroline rose to her feet, slim and unconsciously alluring before him. 'Why need it be hard?' she murmured. 'You sound as though you want to forget it, and neither of us could do that.'

Adam stared at her for a moment, and then pulled

her into his arms. 'Caroline, this is foolish!' he muttered, but he was trembling, too, and Caroline slid her arms round his neck, destroying his attempt to act sensibly. His mouth found hers again, and now his kisses were the passionate demand of a man for a woman, and Caroline responded without thought of resistance. This was Adam, and she loved him, and she wanted to make him aware of it. Adam's self-control was slipping dangerously low; the warmth and intimacy of this charming room were weaving their own spell, and they seemed alone in a wonderful world of their own making.

And then, suddenly, a car door slammed, breaking the stillness. A man's and woman's voices could be heard loudly as they came to the front doors, the sounds echoing harshly in the frosty evening air.

With a groan, Adam reluctantly released her, putting her away from him, running a hand through his short, curling hair. Caroline heaved a sigh, and pressed the palms of her hands to her cheeks.

'Who is it?' she whispered, her cheeks burning from their lovemaking, her full young mouth bare of all lipstick. Adam's eyes softened as he looked at her, then he lifted his shoulders helplessly.

'I think it's John,' he replied. 'My son. And it seems he's brought a guest.'

CHAPTER THREE

CAROLINE gasped at his words. 'Adam!' she exclaimed. 'I—I should go. Could—could I leave without them seeing me?'

Adam frowned down at her. 'Why should you want to do that?' he asked coldly.

'Well, I mean. . .' Caroline groped for words. How could she explain that she might embarrass him by her presence? After all, she was such a nobody.

'You're ashamed of being here with me in what might be termed a "compromising situation",' he accused her, his voice like a whiplash.

Caroline grimaced, and shook her head. 'Oh, Adam, you're completely wrong,' she denied, sliding her arms round his arm and clinging to him. 'It's you I'm thinking of. I don't care about myself, but you're his father.'

Adam looked relieved, and bent his head momentarily to hers, his mouth brushing her lips. 'Then maybe it's just as well they have arrived,' he murmured softly. 'We almost forgot I'm old enough to be yours.'

Caroline looked angrily at him. 'Stop talking like that,' she cried, pressing herself against him, 'age doesn't count between us.'

Adam had no time to answer this because there was the sound of footsteps and the door burst open to admit a tall, slim, dark young man and a dazzling blonde.

'Here we are, Dad!' the young man was carolling when he saw Caroline, still in possession of Adam's arm. 'Oh!' he exclaimed abruptly, halted and looked absolutely astounded. In the awkward pause that followed, Caroline found John's eyes appraising her insolently, while the girl seemed to find Adam fascinating.

Adam released himself from Caroline gently and then crossed the room to greet his son.

'How long are you staying?' he asked, and then turned to the blonde with his casual smile. 'And you are. . .?'

'Toni Landon,' the girl supplied eagerly. 'I've heard such a lot about you, Mr Steinbeck. I'm so thrilled to meet you in person.'

Adam merely nodded. He was completely in control of the situation and Caroline marvelled at his composure. She realised his business training gave him all the confidence he needed.

'We're staying until tomorrow night,' said John, looking at his father. 'That is, if we're not intruding.'

Adam raised his shoulders slightly, ignoring the remark, and turning, drew Caroline forward deliberately.

'I want you to meet my son John and his friend Miss Landon, Caro,' he said, smiling. 'John, Toni, this is Miss Caroline Sinclair.'

His method of introduction was not lost on John and Toni and they exchanged a puzzled glance. Who was this girl? And why did she look at Adam like that?

It was nearly six o'clock and they were all relieved when Mrs Jones came bustling in to find out what was going on; who was staying, etc. After a discussion, she went off to show Toni Landon to her room while John joined his father on the couch. Caroline perched on the edge of an armchair feeling utterly miserable now. Their time together had been so short and she resented the intrusion. Already she was feeling possessive towards Adam.

As Adam and John talked she allowed her mind to drift back over the events of the afternoon. If only John and his girl-friend had not arrived at such an inopportune moment. Who could tell whether Adam would ever allow himself to act that way again? His code of honour might be too strong and besides, he might not want to be put into such an intimate situation.

Mrs Jones brought more tea, beaming at John. He too, was obviously well liked by the buxom house-keeper and Caroline felt quite alone. She took over the business of pouring the tea, however, but when she handed a cup to John she could sense his antagonism towards her. His eyes were cold and unfriendly and Caroline felt even worse. She realised what a shock it must have been to discover her here with his father, virtually alone in the house and obviously not unaware of the fact. He must feel curious, she supposed, and puzzled at this turn of events.

At last, he too rose to go and wash, and Caroline and Adam were left alone again. Adam's eyes were caressing and Caroline left her chair to be near him on the couch.

'Oh, darling,' she breathed, sliding her arms round him, revelling in the feel of his lips against her silky hair. Then with a sigh she said: 'I think I ought to go.'

Adam frowned. 'Why?'

Caroline shrugged her slim shoulders. 'Surely you want to be alone with your son?' she said awkwardly.

'Oh, yes, with that girl trying her best to monopolise

the conversation,' remarked Adam dryly. 'No, thank you, honey. Leave her to John!' He let the pad of his thumb caress the back of her hand lightly. 'You're going to stay and have dinner, as planned, and then afterwards I'll drive you back to town, okay?'

Caroline smiled. 'If you really want me to stay, I'll stay,' she agreed willingly. 'But I'm hardly dressed for dinner, am I? Goodness knows what Miss Landon will wear!'

Adam grinned. 'Caro, my love, you look adorable to me, and I'm the only one you should concern yourself with.'

Caroline chuckled. 'You know you are,' she whispered. 'Oh, Adam, it's so delightful here. I wish they hadn't come.'

Adam's eyebrows ascended. 'Really?' he murmured softly. 'Even though you know what would have happened?'

Caroline shivered. 'I don't think I would object to anything you did,' she confessed quietly. 'I wanted to please you. . .not have you telling me how much older than me you are. Did you really care. . .before they came?'

'No,' he muttered, shaking his head. 'And you did please me, honey.' His mouth met hers and her lips parted automatically. She slid one arm round his neck and caressed the nape where his hair was crisp and vital to the touch. 'God. . .I want you,' he groaned fiercely, his mouth drawing the very strength from her body.

Suddenly, without warning, the door opened and Toni Landon came in. Immediately Caroline released herself from Adam's arms, although his fingers round her wrist prevented her from getting up. Caroline was aware that Toni had witnessed their embrace and that she looked absolutely astounded. It obviously amazed her, as it had done Caroline, that a man like Adam should be interested in a girl like Caroline, even if she was very attractive and had hair like heavy spun silk.

'I'm sorry to intrude,' remarked Toni lightly, but she crossed the floor to the fireside swiftly, obviously not intending to withdraw even so. She was now dressed in a cyclamen caftan. Her blonde hair, which she wore short and curly, gleamed in the lamplight and her cheeks were pale and smooth as alabaster. As she looked half-contemptuously at Caroline's ruffled hair and make-up-less face, Caroline wondered how Adam could regard her so disinterestedly. She was, after all, a woman of his world, whereas Caroline herself was a stranger to his society. Then Caroline found Adam's eyes on her, eloquent with meaning, and her heart pounded uncontrollably.

'Have you been here all day?' enquired Toni, looking at Adam with admiring eyes. He looked so big and broad and powerful lounging on the couch, like a tiger, relaxed yet ready to spring. She was quite aware of what Caroline saw in Adam, his whole personality emanated masculinity, and that, together with his attractive physical appearance, was a challenge to any woman. What she couldn't understand was why a man like Adam, with his opportunities and the choice of almost any woman, should choose a nondescript person like this girl!

'No...we came down this afternoon,' replied Adam, taking out his platinum cigarette case and offering it to Toni. 'Do you smoke?'

'Yes, thank you.' Toni accepted a cigarette and watched Adam as he placed two in his own mouth. He lit hers and then his own from the adjoining lighter and handed one to Caroline, who smiled at him as the touch of his fingers sent shivers down her spine.

'Are you at university?' queried Adam of Toni, drawing on his cigarette.

'Oh, no, I live in Radbury,' replied Toni, smiling. 'I've only known John for about two months. We met at a party, when he could drag himself away from his studies.'

'I rather think that wouldn't be too difficult,' remarked Adam dryly, and Toni laughed.

'I believe you've been out of the country,' she continued, retaining his attention.

'I've been to the United States,' nodded Adam. 'I haven't seen much of John since the summer vac.'

'And did you see much of the States while you were there?' asked Toni interestedly.

'It's not my first visit,' replied Adam, allowing a sliver of ash to fall into the hearth. 'I've seen most of the more well-known parts in my time. I think I prefer California, most of all. Life can be very pleasant down there.'

'I'm sure it can,' exclaimed Toni. 'How I envy you. I'd adore to travel all over the world. As it is the Continent is my limit.' She sighed. 'I adore this place. John tells me you designed it yourself. Are you an architect?'

'Hardly,' he answered with an amused expression. 'I'm glad you like it. I like it, too, but I'm afraid I can't spend as much time here as I would like. My work keeps me pretty busy.'

'I expect it does,' nodded Toni enthusiastically. Then with a faint shrug, she turned to Caroline. 'And what do you do, Miss Sinclair?'

Caroline flushed. 'I work in an office,' she replied quietly, not stating whose office. 'I'm a shorthand-typist. How about you?'

Toni gurgled with laughter. 'Gosh, I don't work,' she exclaimed maliciously. 'I had my season last year and I'm just having fun at the moment.'

Caroline forgot her manners for a moment and replied, just as cattily: 'How boring! What do you do with yourself all day long?'

Adam's fingers tightened round her wrist for a moment, and then before the astonished Toni could think of a reply, he released Caroline and rose to his feet. Crossing to the cocktail cabinet nearby, he said:

'What can I offer you to drink, Toni?'

Toni stood up also and crossed to his side, leaving Caroline alone by the fire. 'Have you some vodka?' she asked, smiling up at him.

Caroline stared into the fire. Already she could feel the twinges of jealousy in her stomach and the thought of this girl being alone here all day Sunday with Adam and John appalled her. She was obviously aware of Adam's attraction and appeared to be quite willing to relinquish John if his father was prepared to take his place.

After giving Toni her vodka, Adam poured a sherry for Caroline and a whisky for himself and then returned to the couch. His eyes were amused as he handed Caroline her sherry and for a moment her earlier happiness returned.

A few minutes later John reappeared, washed and

changed into a dark lounge suit. He helped himself to a Martini and then seated himself on the arm of Toni's chair.

Conversation veered from John's studies at university to the state of the weather, Caroline making a remark only rarely. John, it was obvious, resented her presence and Toni considered her ill-dressed and boring. She was sure that it had not been for her, Adam too would have changed into something more suitable for dinner. Only his nearness made her remain in the room when every instinct in her body cried out for her to leave, immediately.

Dinner was served in a white-panelled dining-room whose golden brocade drapes were drawn back to reveal the fountain, illuminated now by multi-coloured lights. Caroline caught her breath as she gazed at the fairy-like scene and realised anew how far removed from her small world was the world of Adam Steinbeck.

The long refectory table gleamed with silver on white damask and a centrepiece of hothouse roses made a startling splash of colour. The meal that followed was delicious, but Caroline might have been eating sawdust for all the enjoyment she got out of it. She was out of place; she had no real right to be there, not like Toni, who knew what it was all about.

She was glad when it was over and they returned to the lounge to have coffee, liqueurs and cigarettes. Caroline and John now occupied armchairs, while Adam and Toni shared a couch. Caroline was aware that Toni had manoeuvred things this way and was past caring. She just wanted to get away and go home. She didn't care if she was adopting a defeatist attitude. She hated the unveiled hostility.

At half-past nine, Adam said: 'I think it's time Caroline and I set off for town. Will you excuse us? I expect I shall be back in a couple of hours, John.'

'Okay, Dad. Mind how you go. The roads are icy.'

'Right, see you later, then.'

'Yes, Dad. Goodnight, Miss Sinclair.' John's voice was cool to say the least.

'Goodnight, John, goodnight, Miss Landon,' she replied smoothly, and preceded Adam from the room.

Outside the air was freezing and since dinner a thick fog had descended with the suddenness that these things adopt. Even the fountain had been turned off and beyond it nothing could be seen.

'Hell,' muttered Adam, scraping the ice from his windscreen. 'What a night!'

He slid into the car beside her and breathed deeply. 'Caro darling, would you mind very much if I asked you to stay the night? It would be crazy trying to drive to London in this. Besides, tomorrow is Sunday, after all.'

Caroline sighed resignedly. 'I suppose not,' she replied wearily. 'Oh, Adam, I wouldn't have minded at all if we'd been alone, but now. . .' Her voice trailed away and he was aware of just how upset she was.

He slid his arm round her and pulled her to him. 'Darling,' he murmured softly. 'Ignore them. John's resentful, I know, but Toni Landon is nothing to us. Hell, John has a different female in tow every time I see him. Do you think I care what either of them think? God, Caro, this is my house and I want you to stay. You have as much right here as anyone, believe me. But what can I say to them really? They're only spoiled

brats after all.' He grinned and kissed her nose.
'All right?'

'Hm,' she murmured, her depression no longer
uppermost in her mind.

'Good, and as you want to be away from them, we'll
go into my study and leave the lounge to them, hmm?'

'Oh, Adam,' she cried softly, and buried her face
against his warm comforting chest.

Adam held her for a moment longer and then in a
husky voice he said:

'Come on, baggage. Let's get indoors before we
freeze to death.'

'All right,' she said, reluctant to leave the intimacy
of the car. 'I'll have to telephone Amanda though, to
let her know what's going on. She'll be like a mother
hen clucking over her chick when she finds out where
I am.' She laughed and they got out of the car. 'The
couple in the flat below us have a telephone,' she
continued, as they walked into the house. 'They'll let
her know what's going on. They're an elderly couple
and they rarely go out.'

'Good,' Adam nodded, closing the front doors.

'Of course, she'll still worry,' said Caroline, sighing.

'What about?' asked Adam, frowning.

'Can't you guess?' she answered provocatively.

He shrugged. 'Don't worry,' he muttered harshly.
'I'm not intending to sleep with you.'

Caroline raised her shoulders helplessly. 'I'm not
worrying,' she exclaimed softly.

He looked hard at her for a moment and then opened
the door leading to his study.

'Take your coat off, while I go and inform Mrs
Jones,' he muttered, and abruptly left her.

Caroline removed her duffel coat and walked into the room. Compared to the opulent luxury of the rest of the house this room was quite austere. Green carpet covered the floor while red leather armchairs were placed carelessly against the walls which were lined with books or filing cabinets. A broad, polished oak desk occupied the centre of the room and was littered with papers.

Flinging her coat on to a chair, Caroline walked round the desk and seated herself in the swing leather armchair which Adam used when he was using the desk. She smiled lazily to herself as she realised just whose chair she was sitting in. Ruth would never believe it, and nor for that matter would Miss Morgan. Although she loved Adam, it was hard to associate the man she knew with the hard-headed business man he became in the Steinbeck Building and with a sigh she leaned forward and began to gather up the papers scattered so untidily about. As she did so she found she was sorting them and soon had separate piles for banking, loans, land purchases, property holdings, etc. There were also numerous begging letters, letters from charitable organisations and finally his personal correspondence. Working automatically she forgot where she was in the fascination of her occupation. Reading about real estate and demolition contracts and all the comprehensive business which the companies of the corporation covered fascinated her, and she was lost in a world of her own when Adam came back.

He closed the door with a click and her head jerked up in surprise. At once she wondered whether what she had been doing was taboo, and flushing she said:

'I'm afraid I've been tidying up your correspondence. I hope I haven't done anything I shouldn't. Do you mind?'

Adam grinned. 'I guess you're welcome to see any of my correspondence,' he replied easily, coming across and leaning over her chair. Studying her neatly arranged piles of letters, he nodded: 'Very business-like. Would you like to take over as my personal secretary? Miss Freeman from the office comes down here from time to time to clear up the overflow, but otherwise it's chaos.'

Caroline turned her head to look up at him and her silky hair swung against his cheek.

'You're not serious,' she exclaimed. 'Besides, I don't think I could do much work if you were around.'

'Oh! Why?' He sounded teasing and wound her hair round his fingers.

'Don't provoke me,' she said, twisting her head away, and with a soft laugh he straightened up.

'Okay, honey. Now, are you going to phone that flat companion of yours?'

'Gosh, I'd forgotten,' she exclaimed, and leaning over the desk picked up the grey telephone.

'By the way,' he remarked as she dialled the number, 'don't discuss my correspondence with your friends, will you?'

'As if I would!' she cried indignantly, as the number began to ring in the Bensons' apartment.

Adam shrugged. 'You have discussed me with your flat companion, haven't you?' he asked quietly. 'After all, wasn't it she who warned you against my intentions?'

Caroline blushed scarlet. 'All right, darling, but in

future I intend to form my own opinions of people,' and she smiled up at him.

Adam's fingers caressed her shoulder, burning through the thick material of her sweater. 'But not of men,' he murmured, putting his mouth to the side of her neck. 'Your friend might just have been right about me. Is she experienced?'

Caroline giggled. 'Remind me to tell you about Ron Cartwright some time,' she said, laughing, then, 'Oh, hello, Mr Benson.'

The Bensons lived below Caroline and Amanda and had always been good neighbours to the two girls. Both the girls liked the knowledge of the old couple living so near as they could always be called upon to help if necessary.

When Caroline had identified herself, she said: 'Could you give Amamda a message for me, Mr Benson?'

'Do you want to speak to Miss Burchester herself?' asked Mr Benson, who was quite willing to go and get her.

'No. . .that's not necessary,' replied Caroline. 'Anyway, I doubt very much whether she'll be in at the moment. If you could put a note under the door letting her know that I'm staying the night with friends and I won't be home until tomorrow.'

'Right you are, Miss Sinclair,' agreed Mr Benson at once. 'Just leave it to me. Has the fog caused this delay?'

'Yes, isn't it dreadful?' said Caroline, smiling at Adam as he placed a lighted cigarette between her fingers.

'Quite a pea-souper,' said Mr Benson, chuckling,

and after a few more pleasantries Caroline rang off.

She picked up the glass containing a Martini which Adam had placed near her and sipped it appreciatively. She sighed.

'Here I am sitting in the chair belonging to the man who owns Steinbeck,' she exclaimed incredulously. 'It's unbelievable!'

'Why?'

'Adam, have you any idea how different our situations are?' she cried, resting her chin on her hand. 'How would you like to live in a tiny flat with only the minimum to live on?'

'I did once,' he answered surprisingly: 'Did you think I was born rich?'

Caroline shrugged. 'I really know very little about you,' she said. 'Tell me more.'

Adam flung himself into an armchair and looked piercingly at her.

'Are you really interested, Caro?'

'Adam, everything about you interests me,' she said, unashamedly.

'Well: I started with a few pounds when I was about twenty. I bought a piece of land which I got cheaply and which I sold for an immense profit. It was comparatively easily done in those days. Prices weren't the same then as they are today. If you take that small deal and imagine it mushrooming into immense proportions, you have the corporation as it stands today. I took in partners, of course, and we took over smaller companies and amalgamated them into the organisation that is now running at Steinbeck. That's all!'

'All!' she exclaimed. 'It's fantastic. I've read about

these things happening but I never knew that was how you became. . .what you are.'

Adam sighed. 'We bought some property in the States in the last few years and that's partly why I spend some of my time over there. I could delegate a lot of my work to my colleagues, but I enjoy doing it myself, and since Lydia died I have had little else to do.'

'Lydia? Your wife?'

'Correct. She died eight years ago. I suppose you've been told it was leukaemia.'

'Yes,' Caroline nodded.

Adam sighed. 'It's quite true, although honestly I don't think Lydia cared much for living after John was born and we were getting steadily prosperous. I really believe she liked being poor, living in the shabby flat in Kennington which was all we could afford when we first got married.'

He rose to his feet and crossed to the cocktail cabinet. Pouring himself a stiff whisky, he swallowed most of it in one gulp.

'So now you know,' he finished, and replaced his glass on the tray.

'Did you love her very much?' asked Caroline, torturing herself with the question.

'Love?' Adam shrugged his powerful shoulders. 'I married Lydia when I was just twenty. I didn't even know what it was all about in those days. She was five years older than I was and she was very keen. She let me treat her how I liked and then one day she told me she was pregnant. I believed her and we got married almost immediately. John was born twelve months later.'

'Oh.' Caroline bent her head. She was sure he had never told anyone else that before and she wanted to run to him and show him that she cared, cared passionately. But she remained where she was.

'Since then,' he continued slowly, 'I've known a lot of women. But love hasn't entered into it.'

'I see.'

'The women of my acquaintance seem to see the millionaire before the man,' he remarked dryly.

'I don't think that's entirely true,' she answered quietly. 'You underestimate your physical appeal, apart from your personality. It's not your money that I care about.'

He shrugged and looked slightly sceptical. 'Not at all?' he asked softly. 'I find that hard to believe.'

Caroline sighed. 'When I met you in the lift that day I had no idea who you were. You attracted me just as much then as you do now.'

Adam bit his lip. 'I see,' he remarked slowly. 'Doesn't money appeal to you at all?'

'Don't be ridiculous, of course it does,' she replied swiftly. 'I'd be a fool to say otherwise. No one wants to be poor. All I'm trying to say is that money alone does not interest me one iota. When I read about girls, teenage girls, marrying men of seventy or more, it appals me. If you imagine I think of you like that you must be mad.' She shivered. 'I could no more let a man like that touch me than. . .' Her voice trailed away.

Adam looked slightly less disbelieving, but not entirely convinced. 'I do believe you think you're serious,' he murmured, in a half-amused tone.

'I am serious,' she said angrily. 'But you're probably too biased to understand it.'

'Maybe I am,' admitted Adam slowly, staring at her. Then with a shrug he said: 'I meant to tell you earlier, I'm afraid I have to go away again on Monday. Something just cropped up.'

Caroline's legs felt suddenly weak. She didn't want him to go away; perhaps forget all about her!

'How long are you going to be away?' she asked, in a forcedly calm voice.

'Well, I'm not precisely sure, but I guess about five days. I'm flying to New York on Monday morning and I hope to be able to go on to Boston on Wednesday. My mother lives in Boston.'

'Your mother!' Caroline was aghast. She had naturally assumed somehow that his mother was dead. He had never mentioned her before, although actually, apart from today, he had never talked about himself.

'Sure. Didn't you think I had one?' he asked with a smile.

'Well, yes. I just assumed she was dead, somehow.'

'My father died when I was quite a boy,' he remarked, 'but my mother came originally from Ireland and as all her relatives are now living in the States she preferred to be there rather than here, where she never sees me anyway.'

'I see.' Caroline sighed. She had learned such a lot about him today, and there was so much more she wanted to know!

'Will you miss me, then?' he asked teasingly.

'Of course,' she replied, keeping her voice light. 'Who'll help me out when I'm late at the office?'

Adam smiled. 'Would you like me to leave instructions that you can keep what hours you like?'

Caroline flushed. 'Oh, no, I was only joking,' she

exclaimed. 'How I envy you! I'd love to be able to say, I'm flying to the States, just like that.'

Adams eyes narrowed. 'Come with me,' he said coolly.

Caroline's expression mirrored her astonishment. Then with a frown she said: 'Don't make jokes like that, please, Adam.'

'Who's joking?' he retorted. 'I'll make the arrangements if you want to come with me.'

'If!' Carolines stomach plunged. How she would adore to do just that. But she knew she couldn't. It wasn't that simple, even if she was prepared to be so daring. After all, there was Aunt Agnes, Amanda. . . It was entirely unrealistic to even consider such a thing.

'No,' she said at last. 'You knew I'd refuse, didn't you?'

'I guess so,' he said with a sigh, and then there was a knock on the door.

Mrs Jones came in at Adam's call.

'I've just taken supper in to John,' she said, with an apologetic glance, 'and when he asked whether you were back, I had to tell him you hadn't gone. He told me to ask you why you don't join them in the lounge.'

'That's all right, Mrs Jones,' said Adam easily. 'But you tell John that we're quite happy where we are and that we'll see them both in the morning. Right?'

'Yes sir,' Mrs Jones nodded. 'And would you both like some supper, sir? I've a Scotch broth bubbling on the stove just waiting for you to try some, with maybe a roll of French bread.'

'Quite cosmopolitan,' grinned Adam. 'All right, Mrs Jones, you've convinced us. Bring it in.'

The broth was delicious and afterwards they had

creamy coffee made with freshly whipped cream. When they had finished and Mrs Jones came to take the tray, Adam said:

'Did you make up the rose room as I asked you, Mrs Jones?'

'Yes, sir. Just as you said. Miss Landon is in the blue suite.'

'That's right. Perhaps you would show Miss Sinclair to her room.' He turned to Caroline. 'You go along with Mrs Jones, honey,' he murmured softly. 'Goodnight.'

'Goodnight, Adam,' said Caroline, and obediently followed Mrs Jones from the room.

Her bedroom, with its adjoining bathroom, was upstairs and Caroline was absolutely bemused by the splendour of it all. A white pile carpet covered the bedroom floor and one's feet sank in it up to the ankles. The bedding and curtains were rose-coloured satin and the bedhead was quilted. The furniture was a rich mahogany while a white telephone stood on the bedside table.

The bathroom was even more fantastic, with a floor of rich mosaic design, scattered about with thick rugs. The walls were all mirrors, reflecting one hundreds of times over, and Caroline felt sure she would feel embarrassed bathing in such surroundings. The bath, sunken deeply into the floor, was circular, with silver taps and an adjoining shower compartment.

With determination, Caroline turned on the taps and walked back into the bedroom to collect a pair of Adam's pyjamas which were lying on the bed in readiness for her use.

After almost filling the bath and adding some bath

salts she found in the bathroom also, she had a really satisfying bath and got out feeling refreshed. She dried herself on the woolly white bath towels and put on the silk pyjamas. They felt expensive and the dressing gown which had also been supplied could have been wrapped round her twice.

Then she went back into the bedroom and sat down on the bed, unable to consider sleep for a while. She wished she had been able to say more to Adam before she had been shepherded off by Mrs Jones, but perhaps he wanted it that way. She took a cigarette from the box beside the telephone and after lighting it lay back against the pillows luxuriously. This bed for instance, she mused, would sleep about six adults, let alone only one, and that ceiling; who had devised such an intricate system of design? All the opulence seemed so different from the flat she shared with Amanda and she couldn't deny that she preferred this room to the small cubby-hole she and Amanda slept in at home.

She switched off the main lights, leaving only the bedside lamp burning casting a golden glow over the room. Her watch told her that it was half-past eleven and she thought lazily that she ought to be getting right into bed. She stubbed out her cigarette and then lay back again. She felt relaxed and sleepy.

Suddenly there was a light tap on the door and it opened to admit Adam. He closed the door and leaned back against it, smiling.

She sat up, startled at his unexpected entrance. He was still fully dressed and he moved away from the door towards the bed.

'Don't be perturbed,' he murmured lazily. 'I've only

come to make sure you're all right and to say goodnight.'

Caroline sighed. 'I thought you must have wanted me out of the way,' she replied softly.

Adam shrugged. 'Did it sound like that? No, honey, I just didn't want to give Mrs J. anything to gossip about. After all, you're very young...and very beautiful...' He bit his lip savagely as he looked down at her.

'I'm glad you think so,' she answered quietly. She lay back. 'I think this is a wonderful room.'

He did not reply but continued looking at her until she said:

'I suppose these are your pyjamas?' in a husky voice.

'So they are,' he murmured, his eyes caressing her slender body. With a groan he sank down beside her and pulled her into his arms, his mouth seeking hers. There was a tenderness in his kiss which overwhelmed her and then as she responded the kiss hardened and became passionately absorbing.

'Adam,' she breathed achingly, and with a muffled curse Adam wrenched himself away and rose to his feet.

'God, Caro,' he muttered, 'you don't know what you do to me.' He turned away abruptly and thrust his hands into his pockets.

'I know what you do to me,' she protested, propping herself up on one elbow, the revers of the pyjama jacket falling apart to reveal the curve of her firm breast.

Adam glanced once round at her and then he said: 'Go to sleep!' in a forced manner and strode to the door. A few seconds later it slammed behind him and Caroline rolled over on to her stomach and burst into tears.

CHAPTER FOUR

THE next morning Caroline was awakened by Mrs Jones who had brought her a tray on which was a percolator of coffee and a jug of fruit juice. She placed the tray across Caroline as she lazily sat up and then drew back the curtains. A watery sun was shining, but the frost sparkling on the windows gave everything a wintry look.

'Breakfast is in the dining-room when you want it,' she said, smiling. 'Just go along as soon as you want to.'

'Thank you, Mrs Jones.' She sighed. 'This is wonderful.'

Mrs Jones simply nodded and withdrew and Caroline poured herself a glass of fruit juice before tasting the delicious-smelling coffee.

Afterwards, when she was dressed, she went down to the dining-room, finding her way quite easily. The house still seemed very quiet and she wondered whether she was first up. It was eight-thirty already, but for a Sunday it was quite early, even for her.

She looked rather pale this morning, shadows beneath her green cat's eyes. In truth she had slept rather badly and dreaded her eventual meeting with Adam.

When she entered the large, light dining-room she found only one occupant; John Steinbeck, who was seated at the table, a plate of kidneys and bacon in front of him, a newspaper propped against the toast rack.

He looked up at her entrance and looked at her coolly.

'Good morning,' said Caroline, feeling nervous.

''Morning,' he replied abruptly, and rudely returned to his paper.

Ignoring his obviously childish manners, Caroline poured herself more coffee and then seated herself at the opposite side of the table. The dishes being kept hot on burners on the side-board did not appeal to her just now. Her appetite seemed non-existent.

John, apparently deciding he was being very rude and remembering that he was host at the moment, put away the newspaper and offered her some toast.

'No, thank you,' said Caroline, shaking her head.

John finished his kidneys and bacon and buttered himself a slice of toast before spreading it liberally with marmalade. It was obvious now that he also felt rather uncomfortable and Caroline decided to break the silence.

'Is your father still in bed?' she asked politely.

John's eyebrows ascended and he looked cynically surprised.

'Don't you know?' he asked pointedly.

Caroline clenched her teeth for a moment, flushing scarlet.

'If I did I shouldn't be asking,' she replied coldly. 'Now perhaps you'll answer my question.'

Now John looked embarrassed. 'He's going round the estate with Jones,' he said, studying his toast. 'They've been gone over an hour. I ought to have realised that he would hardly be up at seven if. . .' He did not finish his remark, but Caroline was well aware of his meaning.

'You're very young,' she remarked easily, before taking a sip of her coffee.

John looked angry. 'I shouldn't be surprised if I'm older than you,' he retorted with a snort. 'Just what game are you and my father playing? His women aren't usually straight out of the cradle.'

Caroline refused to rise to the bait. Instead she said:

'The fog seems to have lifted this morning.'

John shrugged his shoulders and shook his head. He was baffled. He finished his meal and pushed aside his plate.

'Would you like some more coffee?' Caroline asked, standing up and lifting her own cup.

He was about to refuse and then with ill grace he said:

'Thank you.'

Caroline poured the coffee and after handing him his, re-seated herself. John took out his cigarette case and offered it to her. With a slight smile she accepted the cigarette, steadied his hand as he lit it and then relaxed back in her chair. Even John seemed more at ease and Caroline reflected that in other circumstances she could have liked him. He was young and attractive and quite intelligent and she was sure he could have liked her. Although he was antagonistic towards her, his eyes told her that he found her attractive, too, and she really felt quite amused at his transparent jealousy.

'How long have you been at university?' she asked, drawing on her cigarette.

'A year,' replied John, sounding much more natural. 'I'm reading philosophy.'

'You amaze me,' remarked Caroline with some sarcasm, and John smiled suddenly, relaxing completely. 'Do you like being there?'

'It's okay, I guess,' replied John, with a sigh. 'I quite enjoy the atmosphere, the friends I work with, and of course, I'm interested in my subject.'

'It sounds intriguing,' remarked Caroline. 'I'm afraid philosophy is one subject I know nothing about.'

'Few people do,' replied John, smiling. Then as remembrance of who she was returned to him, he said quietly: 'How long have you known my father?'

'A week,' answered Caroline, watching his reaction.

'Is that all?' he exclaimed, then he shrugged. 'You seem to have become very well acquainted in a very short time.'

Caroline flushed. 'It happens like that sometimes,' she replied calmly.

'So I believe,' said John, with a sneer in his voice. 'And I suppose money doesn't bother you either?'

'No, it does not!' exclaimed Caroline. 'Honestly, it seems to me that far too much emphasis is placed on money in this family. You can please your petty little self whether you believe me or not, but your father's money is not what attracted me to him. He's a very attractive man, or hadn't you noticed? Your girl-friend has!'

John was furious now and Caroline felt pleased. He thought he was so clever. Well, she had shaken his complacency!

She rose to her feet and strolled over to the wide windows which overlooked the drive. It gave John time to control his temper. He had not enjoyed being made a fool of by a girl he was coming to like, regardless of her attachment to his father. He was used to being immediately popular with any girls he met and the fact that this girl preferred his father baulked him. She must know that he was just as attractive moneywise, and he could not understand how she could prefer his father who was almost forty. After all, she could only be about eighteen herself!

The entry of Toni Landon brought a welcome end to his speculation and he turned to greet her with a smile. Dressed this morning in a slim-fitting skirt and a red sweater, she looked very charming and John decided to ignore Caroline.

'I'm sorry I'm late, darling,' she exclaimed. 'You ought not to have such comfy beds here. Mine was dreamy...but dreamy, darling.'

Caroline raised her eyes heavenward as she listened to Toni's inconsequent chatter. No wonder Adam was soon bored if the women of his acquaintance spoke like that. Decorative ornaments, thought Caroline, sighing. Somewhere for the men to hang the jewellery where it would be seen. Walking models of fabulous dresses but inwardly empty shells without any interest in anything but themselves.

Excusing herself, she left the dining-room, collected her duffel coat from the cloakroom and slipping it on opened the front door and stepped outside. Closing the door behind her, she shivered momentarily as the cold air hit her after the heat of the house.

Everywhere was covered with the fairy-like coating of frost and the air was fresh and invigorating. Much different from London, thought Caroline, used to the smells of petrol and diesel fumes. Thrusting her hands deep into the pockets of her coat, she made her way round to the rear of the building where she had seen the swimming pool the night before.

It was easy to find her way and she walked on down the path, through the now stark rose beds, past the pool and the tennis courts into a copse of trees. Her earlier lethargy had partly dispersed when she came out of the trees into a clearing to find a stables, and standing in the forecourt was Adam with two other men. One was obviously the groom and she presumed the second man must be Jones, Mrs Jones' husband.

Adam saw her first and leaving the other men he crossed swiftly to her side. Caroline's cheeks were flushed now from the air, but her eyes were still tired and the dark rings could not be disguised.

Adam did not speak at once, but touched her cheeks lightly, indicating the pallor beneath her eyes.

'Am I to blame for this?' he asked softly, his eyes gentler than she had ever seen them.

'Why should you think that?' she asked, turning away. 'You didn't tell me you kept horses, Adam.'

Adam put a casual arm across her shoulders. 'Don't be frigid with me,' he commanded quietly, and she was forced to look up at him appealingly.

'I'm not,' she breathed helplessly. 'I just don't understand you.'

'You will in time,' he replied calmly. 'Come on, I'll introduce you.'

He introduced her to Frank Leyton, the groom who with his wife and two sons lived over the stables in a converted flat. Mr Jones was a cheerful, older man and she felt quite at home with them both.

The horses were a delight in themselves. Caroline was unable to ride, but she loved animals, and Adam said:

'I'll teach you to ride, next time you come down, hm?'

Caroline sighed contentedly. His final remark had told her all she wanted to know. There was going to be a 'Next time'.

They strolled slowly back to the house together, Adam's arm still across her slim shoulders.

'For the first time in my life, I wish I didn't have to go away tomorrow,' he murmured, his mouth brushing her ear.

'So do I,' she said, sighing and his arm tightened possessively.

They drove up to London after Adam had had some breakfast. He had suggested that she should stay all day, but apart from John's apparent antipathy, Caroline knew that Amanda would be worried so she decided to go back. Adam had been disappointed at her refusals to stay, but he was deliberately thoughtful towards her as they drove back to town.

He drew up outside the block of flats and Caroline bent her head, feeling utterly depressed. The week stretched ahead of her, blank and uninviting.

'Well,' said Adam sliding his arm along the back of her seat, 'our time together is over for the time being.'

Caroline nodded, feeling as though she wanted to cry. She had never felt so miserable or so alone before.

'Oh, Adam,' she whispered, raising her eyes to his, 'you aren't just playing with me, are you?'

Adams eyes darkened. 'Need you ask?' he muttered harshly. 'God, Caro, do you think I want to leave you here? If I had my way, I'd take you with me. But that's not possible, is it?'

'No!' she whispered with a sigh. 'When will you be back?'

'I guess Friday,' he replied, biting his lips. 'I'll ring you at work, hm?' He smiled at her. 'As soon as the flight lands, yes?'

'From the airport!' she exclaimed, smiling herself.

'If you want me to,' he replied softly. 'I'd ring you from New York, but you've no telephone in the flat.'

'Don't worry,' she said. 'Just ring as soon as you get back, darling.'

'Say that again,' he muttered. 'I like to hear you say it.'

Afterwards he lightly touched her forehead with his lips.

'Go on now, honey. Don't say anything else or I really won't let you go,' he said, and she slid out of the car. She felt slightly intoxicated. That kind of conversation was more potent than alcohol. Adam slammed the door and drove away without looking back. Caroline walked slowly into the building. She wished for once she could have a room of her own where she could have gone for a while until the worst of this feeling wore off. As it was, she had Amanda to face. And Amanda would demand a full description of the night's events.

It was almost twelve when she opened the door of the flat and entered to find Amanda preparing dinner. She turned round when Caroline came in, relief spreading over her face.

'Thank heaven!' she exclaimed, looking thankful. 'I thought you were never coming back.'

'Oh, really, Mandy,' cried Caroline, sighing. 'I only stayed at Slayford because of the fog. It was a vile night.'

'I know, I know. But I couldn't help remembering who you were with and wondering whether he would take advantage of such a heaven-sent opportunity.'

'We were not alone,' said Caroline wearily, tiredness overtaking her. 'His son and his girl-friend arrived last night for the weekend. Not to mention his housekeeper and her husband. Honestly, Amanda, don't fuss over me so much. I'm perfectly all right and still sound in wind and limb. Nothing happened.'

Amanda shrugged her shoulders, looking hurt, and Caroline frowned. She didn't want to be unkind to her friend, but at the moment she was in no mood for gossiping. As for her relationship with Adam; she realised that she was like putty in his hands and that Amanda would have been shocked to the core if she ever realised it. Caroline knew she had never felt like this before, and was not likely to do so again with any other man. Up till now, boys had hardly disturbed the surface of her emotional state, suddenly Adam had plumbed the depths and she felt shaken at the upheaval he had caused. Would he ever feel the same way towards herself? She doubted it. He had known too many women to get himself seriously involved with a teenager.

If Amanda wondered why Caroline was so miserable for the rest of the day she did not comment on it and refrained from asking any questions. It was obvious that Caroline did not want to talk about things concerning Adam Steinbeck and Amanda had to resign her curiosity and forget all the things she would have liked to have known.

The week that followed seemed the longest of Caroline's life. She went to work automatically, just living for the weekend and Adam's return. Ruth, who questioned her about Adam, received monosyllabic replies and soon tired of asking. Caroline felt sure Ruth thought she was a misery and she tried to be her usual cheerful self without much success.

The weather was cold and miserable too, and as it was only the middle of December everybody was forecasting a long, hard winter. Caroline listened to the old men on the bus grumbling about the inadequacy of their pensions to provide coal or heating of any kind and she thought how lucky she really was to be young and still able to work. Although she and Amanda thought their lives were dull, compared to some theirs was an ideal existence and she resolved to be more tolerant in future and more cheerful. After all, it was Thursday already and Adam was due back tomorrow.

Mark Davison came into the typing pool on Thursday afternoon with a sheaf of letters for one of the other girls. After delivering them and seeing that Miss Morgan was not about he strolled across to Caroline's desk. A tall, slim, fair young man dressed in a light grey suit, he looked debonair and quite handsome, and was well aware of it.

He leaned on Caroline's desk, familiarly, and said:
'Hi, gorgeous!'

Amused at his rather old-fashioned line of introduction, Caroline smiled. 'What do you want?' she asked. 'Miss Morgan will be back any minute and you know she doesn't like you lingering in here any longer than is necessary.'

'Oh, but this is necessary,' replied Mark airily. 'Besides, the old dragon is closeted with Mr Willis, so she won't be back for quite some time. Now... what's this crazy story I hear about you having lunch with the boss man?'

Caroline shrugged. The story was gradually circulating round the whole building.

'That was last week,' she remarked coolly. 'It's quite old news now.'

'Maybe,' said Mark, raising his eyebrows. 'But it's still pretty hot stuff, isn't it? My, my, we are playing for high stakes. No wonder yours truly isn't even in the running.'

'Don't be ridiculous, Mark,' Caroline retorted, feeling angry now. It was one thing for people to gossip about what had actually taken place. It was quite another for them to speculate on what might happen in the future. She didn't like the idea of Adam's name being bandied about like that. It had never happened before and Mark's manner of speaking brought it home to her how enjoyable other people found this kind of tit-bit about an influential man.

'I don't think it is ridiculous,' replied Mark easily, a mocking smile on his face. 'After all, darling you're hardly in his class, are you? I mean, whatever there is between you two can only be thought the worst of, can't it? Even you can't imagine anything serious might come of it.'

'It was only lunch,' said Caroline, grateful that no one knew of the weekend affair.

'At the moment,' nodded Mark, thoughtfully lighting a cigarette. 'But you know what it's like when you cast a stone into a still pond, the ripples spread, don't they?' He saw Caroline looking rather perturbed, and seizing his opportunity, he continued: 'Of course, you could squash the rumours.'

'How?' she asked eagerly, unaware of his thoughts.

'By going out with somebody else. After all, a girl who's already dating one boy doesn't bother with a man old enough to be her father.'

Suddenly what he was getting at came through to her. 'I suppose you mean I should go out with you?' she said with a sigh.

'Now that's a great idea,' he said, grinning. 'How about it?'

Hating him for his over-confident manner and boyish lack of imagination. Caroline hesitated. But Mark Davison was quite a talker himself and she could imagine him making the most of this if she refused. Caught between the devil and the deep blue sea, she capitulated.

'All right, then,' she said, forcing her voice to sound light and cheerful. 'When would you suggest?'

'How about this evening?' answered Mark eagerly. He was jubilant. He had never expected it to be this easy.

Caroline agreed. After all, she thought, tomorrow she might conceivably be seeing Adam. After Mark had gone she did not feel so keen. It was all very well going out with that big-headed creature to stop tongues from wagging, but what if Adam thought she was turning to someone else behind his back? Then she sighed. Why should she even believe that Adam might care? Her position was so uncertain at the moment.

By five o'clock she was regretting her decision, but she met him in the foyer as arranged and there was no backing out. They went to the cinema to see a biblical epic. The cinema was in the West End and Caroline quite enjoyed the unexpected treat. Although he had only tried to hold her hand in the cinema, Caroline was dreading going home with him in case he started to get fresh. It wasn't that she couldn't handle him. She simply did not want to offend him. He might spread more stories about herself and Adam.

Before going home they had supper in a Chinese restaurant and Caroline toyed disinterestedly with her chicken chop suey. She was not in the mood for conversation and Mark was a veritable chatterbox. He seemed satisfied with her short replies, however, and she hoped he thought she was enjoying herself.

Outside the restaurant Mark hailed a taxi, but Caroline protested.

'Really, I'm quite capable of getting the bus home,' she exclaimed. 'I don't mind going alone and it will be so late if you come with me.'

'I don't care,' replied Mark determinedly, and as a taxi drew to a halt he helped her in and climbed in after her.

She sat as far away from him as possible in the back seat and Mark, after one abortive attempt to put his arm round her, left her alone. The taxi stopped in Gloucester Court and Mark paid the driver as he climbed out. Caroline sighed wearily. He obviously intended making a prolonged goodnight.

When the taxi had gone she walked towards the steps leading into the flats.

'Well,' she said firmly, 'thank you for a lovely evening. Goodnight.'

'Wait a minute,' exclaimed Mark. 'You're not going in yet?'

'I'm afraid I am,' she replied, turning to face him. 'What's your idea?'

'Well, a kiss for a start,' said Mark, and pulled her forcefully towards him.

Caroline turned her face from side to side, avoiding his seeking lips, trying to release herself.

'Let me go,' she cried angrily. 'Just who do you think you are?'

'Relax,' he snapped, angry himself. He was not used to this reaction.

'I will not!' Caroline wrenched herself away. 'You must be crazy,' she said furiously. 'Men don't force their attentions on girls these days. You just haven't grown up, have you, Mark?'

'I guess you must prefer older men,' he retorted sarcastically. 'But sister, you're welcome to them. I wouldn't touch you again with a bargepole.'

'You wouldn't get the chance,' she exclaimed hotly.

'Why? Are you still angling for the great man himself? You've got some hopes! And when he hears you've been out with me he won't be so interested.'

Caroline clenched her fists and with a muffled sob, she turned and ran into the building.

The following day Caroline spent in expectation, waiting for a call from Adam. Every time the office telephone rang she longed to rush and answer it, but when someone else did and it was not Adam she was glad she had remained seated. She did not want to make an exhibition of herself.

At lunch time she ate very little and Ruth noticed this.

'What's wrong?' she asked. 'Are you sickening for something?'

Caroline smiled. 'Of course not. I'm not very hungry, that's all.'

Ruth shrugged. 'Your appetite certainly seems to have deteriorated of late,' she remarked. 'You're surely not slimming or anything ridiculous like that, are you?'

Caroline chuckled. 'No, I'm not slimming. I guess people have these spasms of not eating from time to time.'

'I wish I did,' wailed Ruth. 'My waistline is definitely thickening. I really will have to start slimming in earnest.'

'You're all right,' said Caroline, looking at her friend critically. 'It's probably getting very little exercise that has made you fatter. You'll have to get a bicycle and ride to work.'

'Some chance!' exclaimed Ruth, laughing. 'But we're getting away from you again. How did the date with Mark go down?'

'Don't mention it,' said Caroline, shivering. 'He's awful. However, he didn't get far with me.'

'He must be slipping,' remarked Ruth with a grimace. 'I know him of old. I used to go out with him when I first started here.'

'Did you really? He seems to date everyone.'

'At least,' said Ruth dryly, 'he has a name like mud.'

'You never told me that,' exclaimed Caroline, frowning.

'I thought you knew,' exclaimed Ruth. 'Good heavens, Caroline, surely you've heard the tales about Mark Davison? Some say one girl left because she was expecting his kid and he abandoned her. Anyway, she lost the kid and nearly died. That was ages ago, of course.'

Caroline felt nauseated. And this was the man she had gone out with to divert attention from Adam! What hornets' nest of trouble had she stirred up for herself?

'I'm going back to the office,' she said, standing up.

Ruth looked puzzled. 'Okay, Caroline. I'll be along in about five minutes.'

'Don't hurry,' replied Caroline, and walked swiftly away.

Adam did not telephone all afternoon and by evening Caroline felt dreadful. A fog had descended again when she got outside the building and she hoped Amanda would be out when she got home. She had told Amanda that Adam was coming home on Friday and she would be sure to ask questions.

For once fate seemed to be on her side and Amanda had left a note saying that she had had an invitation to a party and had accepted, seeing that Caroline would probably be tied up with Adam Steinbeck.

Caroline read the note and then tore it up and threw the pieces into the waste paper basket. Some hopes, she thought wryly, and trying to ignore the ache in her heart she took off her coat and walked into the bedroom.

Jim Mercer ground the stub of his cigarette into the floor of the VIP lounge with his heel and looked regretfully at Adam.

'Well,' he said with a grimace, 'that last announcement settles it, doesn't it?'

Adam thrust his hands deep into the pockets of the thick, fur-lined overcoat he was wearing and shrugged his broad shoulders impatiently. A cold airport was hardly his choice of an afternoon's entertainment and he was cold and angry.

'Yes,' he said abruptly, in reply to his personal assistant's statement. Then with a last draw on his own cigar he dropped it too and said: 'Do you realise we've been hanging about this place since six o'clock this morning? It's now two o'clock, that's eight hours, Jim.'

'Yes, sir, I know.'

'I wanted to be back in London today, do you realise that? Even if there was a flight now it would be tomorrow before we get there.'

'Yes, sir. But the met. office seems to think the fog won't lift for at least another six hours.'

'I know, I know. So they've booked us hotel accommodation. All right, Jim, I have ears, too, you know.'

'Yes, sir.' Jim felt uncomfortable. He had enjoyed this visit with Adam and had enjoyed visiting his mother in Boston. Most of all he had enjoyed meeting Adam's cousin, Virginia. She was only twenty-three and had obviously liked him too. Perhaps if he hadn't been enjoying himself so much they might have flown home yesterday and thus avoided this blasted fog. Who could tell what Adam was thinking? And anyway, why was he so keen to get back to England? He never had been before, and Jim had been all over the world with him.

Now Adam forced a wry smile and patted Jim on the shoulder.

'Come on,' he said. 'I guess I'm making a lot of fuss. Let's you and me find a bar and have ourselves a few pick-me-ups, hm?'

'That's a great idea,' said Jim with a grin, and they left the comparative luxury of the lounge for the public bar.

Later, as he relaxed in a hot bath before having dinner, Adam allowed himself to wonder what Caroline would be thinking. He could not ring her now. It was too late, and apart from that a call from New York could not be made without causing a lot of publicity at both ends. It was very unfortunate. Perhaps the fog was also stifling London and she would guess what had happened.

They eventually left New York late in the evening and arrived in London at nine-thirty in the morning, London time. Adam decided to drive straight to the office and clear up any necessary correspondence before the building closed for the weekend. He knew that Caroline worked alternate Saturday mornings and as she had not worked last week this should be her morning in. However, a brief call, before leaving the airport informed him that Caroline had not turned up that morning. Inwardly cursing, Adam returned his thoughts to business commitments and was silent in the chauffeur-driven Rolls which a cable had brought to the airport to meet them, and which drove Adam and Jim Mercer to the Steinbeck Building.

Laura Freeman was waiting in her office when he strode through the door of her domain, Mercer at his heels. She looked excessively pleased with herself, and so she should, she thought delightedly. She had always wanted Adam Steinbeck, to no avail, and when she found out that he had taken a junior typist to lunch she had been furious. And then, yesterday morning, she had met Mark Davison in the staff canteen and their conversation had cheered her up considerably. If Caroline Sinclair was going out with someone like Mark Davison, there could be nothing between her and Adam. Adam had always disliked Davison because of his over-clever manner, but being unable to find fault with his work he allowed him to remain on sufferance. If he just happened to hear about it, accidentally, as she intended he should, he might possibly be interested in finding someone else!

''Morning, Miss Freeman,' said Adam, crossing her office, removing his overcoat as he did so. Mercer made a grimace at Laura and she smiled in return. 'Bring in your notebook,' continued Adam, entering his own office and walking over to his desk. There was a pile of correspondence awaiting his perusal and before doing anything else he quickly flipped through the letters. He pinpointed some for his immediate attention and then flung the rest into an 'Incoming' basket and handed them to Jim.

'I think you can deal with these, Jim,' he said brusquely. 'Some this morning, the rest next week. Right?'

'Right, sir. Do you want me to stay?'

'No, you can get along. I'll see you on Sunday at the villa.'

'Yes, sir. Good morning.'

Jim withdrew as Laura came in and seated herself opposite Adam. Adam lit himself a cigar and studied the first letter with interest. Soon he was dictating briskly, and Laura was kept completely alert to stay with him.

In a lull between letters, Laura spoke: 'Did the fog delay you, sir?' she asked politely.

'Yes,' replied Adam shortly. 'Shall we get on?'

The next half-hour sped by and at last Adam called a halt. 'I think that will do,' he said, relaxing somewhat. 'Could you get me some coffee, Miss Freeman? I could do with some.'

'Of course.' Laura withdrew and returned ten minutes later with a tray.

Adam accepted the cup she handed to him, and then said:

'Anything special I should know? Did the grant come through for the Marsden deal?'

'Yes, sir. Mr Willis dealt with it directly.'

'Good, good. By the way, Miss Sinclair isn't in this morning. Do you know why? I believe this is her week to work Saturday morning.'

'Yes, it is,' agreed Laura, hardly daring to believe her luck. What a heaven-sent opportunity this was! 'Perhaps she's ill,' she suggested quietly. 'I know she was all right on Thursday night because she was out with Mark Davison. I was speaking to him yesterday in the canteen and he was telling me all about the film they'd seen.' There, she had said it!

If she had expected Adam to show some reaction she was disappointed. He merely shrugged and said: 'Perhaps the 'flu bug has bitten her. It's certainly been very cold.'

He finished his coffee and rose to his feet. 'Well, Miss Freeman, I'll leave you to get on. It's bed for me. I haven't seen one since Thursday night and I'm dead on my feet.'

Amanda came out of the bedroom wearing her new red coat.

'How do I look?' she asked of Caroline, who was lounging moodily in a chair, smoking a cigarette and leafing idly through a fashion magazine.

Caroline looked up. 'Fine,' she said, but there was no enthusiasm in her voice.

'Oh, do buck up,' exclaimed Amanda. 'It's Saturday night and here you are lounging about in those old jeans. Look, why don't you come with us? Bobby won't mind. He's divine, and besides, it's a party. There'll be heaps of boys.'

Bobby was Amanda's new boy-friend and tonight they were going to one of the interminable parties which Amanda seemed to enjoy. Caroline felt sure they would bore her to death and told Amanda so.

'You're getting quite morbid,' said Amanda angrily.

'No, I'm not,' said Caroline, sighing. 'I'm tired. I'm going to have a bath and then I'm going to bed.'

'Oh, well. I'm going,' said Amanda crossly. 'Have fun,' and she went out, slamming the door.

After she had gone, Caroline flung the magazine across the room with an angry exclamation. Why, oh, why didn't Adam get in touch with her? Why didn't he let her know what was going on?

She stood up and walked restlessly round the room. She felt so fed-up and miserable. If only he would come!

At eight o'clock she decided to wash her hair and have her bath and as everyone else seemed to be either out or engrossed with their television sets she had plenty of time to take it slowly.

The bathroom was on a lower floor than their flat and it was nearly nine o'clock when she returned to their rooms wrapped in her quilted housecoat, over her nightdress. She put on the kettle to make some coffee and then curled up on the couch in front of the electric fire to dry her hair. Her hair was still damp and clinging to her cheeks in tendrils when there was a knock at the door of the flat.

Trembling slightly and her heart pounding, Caroline crossed the room.

'Who is it?' she asked without unlocking the door.

'Steinbeck,' came the deep voice she had been longing to hear.

'Adam!' she exclaimed, and flung open the door, stepping back to allow him to enter. He looked bigger and broader and more attractive than ever in his thick overcoat and dark suit. For a moment she just allowed herself the pleasure of looking at him; she had been needing this so much.

Then she closed the door and leaned back against it. Whether she had expected him to take her in his arms, she wasn't sure, but she was not at all prepared for his solemn expression and the slight trace of mockery behind his eyes.

'Hello, Caroline,' he said, nodding, his eyes never leaving her face.

Feeling conscious suddenly of her dishevelled appearance, she said:

'I'll go and get dressed,' but before she could move his fingers curved round her wrist.

'Don't bother,' he said smoothly. 'I shan't be staying long. Go and sit down.'

Shrugging, Caroline resumed her position on the couch while Adam loosened his overcoat and walked lazily towards the fire. He looked very attractive to Caroline and her stomach was churning with a strange fear she could only guess at.

'Were you late in getting home last night?' she asked, looking up at him.

'Last night?' Adam raised his eyebrows. 'No, the fog delayed the flight and it was early this morning before we landed in London.'

'Oh, I see.' Caroline half-smiled. That at least partly explained the lateness of his visit. Her heart lightened a little, but Adam's expression was not encouraging.

'You weren't in at the office this morning,' he said quietly.

'No. I'm sorry. I didn't sleep too well last night and I felt rotten when I got up.'

Adam nodded, and drew out his cigarette case. Caroline accepted a cigarette and a light and then waited impatiently for his next words.

'I simply came to say goodbye,' he said calmly.

Caroline's face went pale. 'What!' she exclaimed, suddenly shivering.

Adam shrugged and drew on his cigarette. 'You must have known it would end some time,' he remarked easily.

Caroline did not trust herself to speak. She merely shook her head in bewilderment. This was not the Adam who had gone away. The same man with whom she had shared last weekend. She suddenly realised that she had been afraid all week that something like this might happen and that was why, although she had known he would be home at the weekend, she had felt so miserable.

He put his hand in his pocket and drew out a flat box and dropped it into her lap. 'I brought you a present,' he murmured. 'From New York.'

Caroline's fingers trembled as she opened the lid. Inside, gleaming magnificently on white velvet, lay an inch-wide bracelet of platinum set with emeralds, rubies and diamonds. It was the most beautiful and expensive piece of jewellery she had ever seen, but her heart and stomach were sickened. Did he imagine he had to pay her off? She snapped the box shut and held it out.

'I'm afraid I can't accept it,' she said coldly. 'If it's meant to be a memento of our...well... association...it...it's not necessary. I prefer to buy my own jewellery, thank you.'

It was hard to sound aloof when you were crying inside and Caroline's voice was rather unsteady, for all its touch of dignity.

Adam merely took the box and placed it on the mantelshelf.

'You'll change your mind,' he remarked dryly, unconvinced of her sincerity.

Caroline rose to her feet. 'How dare you suggest such a thing!' she gasped furiously. 'Do you imagine that because I don't live in luxury, I'll grab every hand-out that comes my way? You must have a very low opinion of me.'

'Not of you,' he replied smoothly. 'At least not particularly. I find women in general are much of a kind.

'Well, I'm not that kind,' she stormed. 'You can take your bracelet and give it to someone who really will appreciate it. Someone who will be only too pleased to do anything you ask them, simply because you're the great Adam Steinbeck!'

'You're very young,' was all he said.

Caroline felt helpless. This kind of arguing was getting them nowhere. She didn't want him to think of her as a little spitfire. She wanted him to want her! To love her! Why was he suddenly so cold and remote? There had got to be a reason.

She clenched her fists. 'Are you saying all this because I'm too young?' she asked, with a sigh. 'Surely I have a right to know.'

Adam shrugged his broad shoulders.

'Something of the kind,' he agreed in that infuriatingly cool tone.

Caroline turned away and ran her hands round her neck and under her hair at the back. 'You certainly have changed,' she said achingly. 'You really had me fooled.'

'I might say the same thing about you,' he replied, buttoning his overcoat. He strolled to the door.

'You've forgotten your bracelet,' she said, a lump in her throat.

'Your bracelet,' he corrected her and let himself out of the flat.

CHAPTER FIVE

THE next day was, of course, Sunday, and Caroline woke late feeling utterly depressed. She had never felt so unhappy and life seemed uninteresting and uninviting. She lay in bed, feigning sleep, until lunch time, allowing Amanda to get up alone. She dreaded facing her and the barrage of questions that would have to be answered. She supposed she was a coward, but this had been the most important thing in her life and now it was gone. She still could hardly believe the happenings of the previous evening and she hoped they had only been a bad dream.

Amanda douched this hope when she came in about twelve o'clock carrying the box containing the bracelet.

'Is this yours?' she exclaimed with a smile, when she saw Caroline's eyes were open.

'No,' replied Caroline shakily, tears welling up in her eyes. 'It belongs to Adam Steinbeck. He forgot to take it with him last night. I'll have to return it to him.'

Amanda frowned. 'Honey, I know I'm an inquisitive blighter, but why are you crying? He came, didn't he? He didn't...well...' Her words and their meaning were perfectly clear.

'He hasn't seduced me,' replied Caroline flatly, 'if that's what you're hinting at. Quite the reverse. Our little affair, to use the term loosely, is over. Don't ask me why. I just don't understand it myself.'

Amanda perched on the end of her bed. 'Perhaps he's been hearing stories about you and this Mark Davison you went out with. That kind of news travels swiftly.'

Caroline sat up abruptly. Until now that thought had not occurred to her. She had told Amanda what a horrible reputation he had, and Amanda had advised her to have nothing more to do with him.

'Oh, Amanda,' she exclaimed, 'do you think it's possible? He went into the office yesterday because he asked why I was absent. But who would want to tell him tales like that, the minute he was home?'

'Maybe somebody else is interested in him, honey,' remarked Amanda shrewdly. 'Your date with lover-boy was asking for trouble. I honestly don't know why you went. It served no useful purpose whatsoever.'

Caroline sighed. 'I told you, I was only thinking of Adam.'

'Even to my ears that sounds a likely tale,' said Amanda gloomily. 'Or should I say unlikely?'

Caroline groaned. 'Amanda, what can I do?'

'I should let that be an end of it,' said Amanda solemnly. 'Really, Caroline. You're better out of it altogether.'

'I'm not, I'm not,' cried Caroline achingly. 'Amanda, I love him.'

Amanda sighed heavily, staring at her friend. 'Are you serious?'

'Never more so,' replied Caroline, burying her face in her hands.

'My God!' Amanda was completely flabbergasted. 'Well, kid, good luck! You're going to need it.'

'But anyway, Mandy, why not tell me about this

business with Mark? Why did he just clam up like that?'

'Look, honey. Steinbeck is nearly forty, you're seventeen.'

'Nearly eighteen,' contradicted Caroline quickly.

'Okay, even so, it's a hell of a difference. Anyway, Steinbeck goes away. Four days later you're out with a boy of nearer your own age. What would you think? I'd think you wanted Steinbeck for his money and Mark Davison for something else.'

'Amanda! Heavens, Adam is much more attractive than Mark Davison! He's the most attractive man I've ever met.'

'Honey, you're biased.'

'Maybe one day you'll see him too, and then you'll know,' replied Caroline. 'Oh, Amanda, what can I do? I've got to do something.'

'I should let things slide for the time being,' replied Amanda slowly. 'You know what they say about absence making the heart grow fonder.'

Caroline sighed. 'Maybe you're right. But I shall send that bracelet back tomorrow. Whatever happens I don't want it.'

On Monday morning, Caroline put the jewel box containing the bracelet in her shoulder bag and took it to work. She could only hope Adam would be in that day, thus enabling her to send the bracelet back via a messenger. She did not want to take it to him herself, but as she sat in the bus on her way to the Steinbeck Building she realised she could hardly send anything as valuable as that with the messenger boy. If it should get lost! Or stolen! Her stomach plunged sickeningly.

No! She would have to deliver the thing herself to his office. If she left it with his secretary she would be sure of it arriving safely.

When she asked Miss Morgan for permission to go up to the chairman's suite, her senior looked astonished. She did not dare refuse her request, however, as she did not know just what the situation was between Caroline and Adam Steinbeck. It was most irregular and most humiliating to have to subordinate herself to an inferior.

'Mr Steinbeck won't be in this morning,' said Miss Morgan tersely.

'That's quite all right,' replied Caroline quietly. 'His secretary will do in this instance.'

'Oh, very well. It's already nine-thirty, and as your coffee break begins in fifteen minutes you had better go now.' She felt and sounded frustrated.

'Thank you,' Caroline smiled, and then turned away to get her handbag.

The lift took her up to the twelfth floor and she stepped out on to the pile-carpeted corridor. Each door indicated its occupant in small gold letters and she had no difficulty in finding 'Steinbeck'.

She knocked and entered Laura Freeman's office, but to her surprise the room was empty. However, there were signs of Laura's occupation, so she surmised that the secretary would not be long in all probability.

There was another door opening off the room, which presumably led to Adam's office. It was closed and Caroline wondered what was beyond. She looked about her nervously, smoothing her shining hair and the heavy red woollen material of her slim-fitting dress. A mirror hung on one wall and she walked across to it and peered at her reflection. She was sure Adam's secretary would be very chic and efficient and she didn't want to appear gauche or untidy.

Her large green eyes looked back at her and she sighed as she remembered again her last meeting with Adam. Her eyes reminded her of her purpose here. They still looked rather hollow, giving her face a haunting beauty.

Suddenly, she had the feeling that someone was watching her and she swung round guiltily. Then she flushed. Adam himself was leaning against the jamb of the door through which he had just entered, regarding her intently. He had obviously just arrived in the building as he was still wearing his overcoat. His almost animal magnetism reached out to her and she shivered. She had never believed one man could ever affect her in this way. Her bones seemed to melt into water at his glance. His eyes on her were broodingly intense and she moved uncomfortably, twisting the box containing the bracelet between her fingers.

After what seemed like an eternity, he straightened up and walked into the room.

'Did you want to see me?' he enquired, his voice curt.

'Well, yes and no,' she replied awkwardly. 'I merely came to return your bracelet. I intended leaving it with your secretary, but she wasn't here. I've been waiting for her.'

Adam looked thoughtful. 'We can't talk here,' he said abruptly. 'Miss Freeman will be back at any moment. Come into my office.'

Passing her, he opened his office door and allowed her to precede him into the room beyond. As she passed him, brushing against his chest, she felt her heart pounding and it was all she could do to prevent herself from pressing herself against him.

His office reminded her of his study at Slayford, except that the wide windows revealed the roofs of London instead of the gardens of his home.

Adam closed the door, and taking off his coat he hung it near the door on an ebony stand. Then he crossed to his desk, flipping over some confidential letters which were awaiting his inspection.

Caroline stood awkwardly in the centre of the room, unaware of what to do next. She felt like a schoolgirl again, up before the headmaster.

'Don't worry,' remarked Adam, glancing up at her. 'This room is soundproof, so no one can hear our conversation. And no one will enter without permission from me.'

Caroline looked down at the toes of her shoes. Then with a stiffening of her shoulders she looked up at him again. Today he was wearing a dark blue suit and matching waistcoat and looked every inch the business tycoon he was.

'So you came to return the bracelet?' he observed, thrusting his hands into the pockets of his trousers.

'Yes. I suppose that's all, then. I've already done what I came to do.' She placed the bracelet on the side of the desk behind which he was standing.

Adam gave her a studied glance. 'On Saturday evening I was rather rude. I apologise.'

'That's quite all right.' Caroline's voice was cool.

'I'm not in the habit of doing that sort of thing,' he continued. 'I suppose I did it very badly?'

'I think you did it very well,' replied Caroline, in an

aloof tone. 'You made your position perfectly clear.'

Adam's eyes narrowed slightly and he shrugged. 'I see. Well, I'm sure it won't be difficult for you to find yourself another escort. I believe there is a young man in this building in whom you are interested.'

Caroline stiffened. So he did know about Thursday evening!

'Do you mean Mark Davison?' she asked angrily.

Adam seated himself behind his desk in the deep armchair: He looked assured and sophisticated and Caroline wanted to break down the barrier he had put up between them.

'I believe that is the young man's name,' agreed Adam easily, lighting a cigar with casual movements.

'I thought it would be,' exclaimed Caroline. 'Who told you about him?'

Adam raised his eyebrows. 'As it's true I hardly think that matters,' he replied slowly. 'He took you to the cinema last week, while I was in the States.'

'Yes, he did. I intended telling you, but I haven't had the chance.'

'Oh, did you?' Adam sounded disbelieving.

'Yes, I did.' She sighed. 'Oh, what's the use! You won't believe me whatever I say.'

'Let's say I already know what you were going to say,' he drawled infuriatingly.

Caroline bent her head. He was so stubborn. She was at a loss to make him see reason. Of course it sounded bad, but sometimes things happened that way.

'Look, Caroline,' he said suddenly, 'I have something to say to you. Sit down.'

'Don't bother,' she retorted, and turned away.

'I said sit down,' he commanded, and with a helpless

shrug she subsided into the seat opposite him.

'Now, listen to me. You might think it's only jealousy that has caused the rift between us and I want to make it clear that it's not. Sure, when I heard about you and Davison I was mad, flaming mad, and jealous too. The minute my back was turned there you were, out with some other kid. Okay, that was that. Maybe you had your reasons. But it made me realise that you're only seventeen, and at seventeen you can't be expected to remain faithful to one man. You want good times, young people to associate with, and I could not and would not want you between dates with other young men. Now do you understand? It's for your own good. You proved when you went out with Davison that you need entertainment all the time. Not just when I can give it to you.'

'You're wrong,' she cried, twisting her fingers together. 'Adam, it wasn't like that! Let me explain!'

'What can you explain? That it was just a flash in the pan? That you'll be a good girl from now on? Let's face it, Caro, I'm too old for you. You're not interested in settling down yet, and I guess that was what I had in mind.'

Caroline burst into tears. To hear him saying that he had wanted her to that extent and now knowing everything was finished almost broke her heart.

'What does age matter when you love somebody?' she whispered brokenly.

'You don't love me...or anyone,' he retorted. 'Caro, I'm just a big adventure to you. You don't want to be serious. And I'm afraid I do.'

'You told me before you went away...well...you know what you said.'

'And I meant it,' he muttered, standing up restlessly. 'God, Caroline, I haven't changed. I've simply come to my senses. Probably this affair has been the best thing that could happen, for you at least.'

Caroline dried her eyes. She felt awful. 'You can't have cared much, either way,' she protested, half to herself, and Adam angrily stubbed out his cigar.

'Stop saying that,' he said angrily. 'Look, I'm leaving for the Caribbean in three weeks' time, on the yacht. When I get back you'll have forgotten all about me and you'll thank me for this.'

Caroline looked up at him. How she longed to be going with him. How could he believe she was so fickle? Why, oh, why had she allowed Mark Davison to talk her into such a crazy thing? Looking at him, his dark eyes holding hers, she felt her senses stirring with the primitive emotions he aroused in her.

'Oh, Adam,' she breathed. 'Don't make this the end, *please*!'

Adam bit his lip. The warmth of her beauty, the haunting unhappiness in her eyes were doing strange things to him and his willpower was being sapped by his physical need of her.

'Do you think I wanted it this way?' he snapped harshly, moving round the desk to her chair.

She rose deliberately to her feet so that her body was touching his. Her instinct seemed to tell her that her nearness would overcome his strength. With a groan he pulled her to him, parting her mouth with his own, and her arms slid round his neck compulsively. Words were unneccessary for the next few minutes and Caroline was breathless and clinging to him when there was a knock at the door. For seconds longer their mouths clung together and then reluctantly he put her away from him, smoothing his ruffled hair, where Caroline's fingers had entwined.

Caroline herself smoothed her own hair, and said: 'Ought I to go?'

Adam shook his head and called, 'Come in.'

Laura Freeman entered, and when she saw Caroline her eyes widened in astonishment which turned to envy when she noticed Caroline's bare mouth and flushed complexion. It was obvious what had occurred and she felt furious that her plan had not worked.

Adam was seated on the edge of his desk. He looked calm and composed and Caroline wondered what this frigid-looking secretary of his would think if she knew just how passionately he had been making love seconds before. Laura Freeman was all she had expected and more, and Caroline could sense Laura's hostility towards herself. With unexpected intuition she felt sure that it had been this woman who had told Adam about Mark Davison.

'I wondered if you were ready to do the letters, Mr Steinbeck,' said Laura, with a forced smile. 'I'm afraid I didn't know you were engaged.' She looked coldly at Caroline.

Adam also looked at Caroline, rather wryly she thought, but she refused to meet his eyes.

'No,' said Adam slowly, dragging his eyes away from Caroline. 'Could you wait a few minutes, Miss Freeman? I'll ring when I'm ready.'

Laura stifled her annoyance. 'Of course, sir,' she replied politely, and withdrew, closing the door with a definite click.

Caroline looked thoughtfully across at Adam.

'Have we shocked her?' she asked, half amused.

'Very probably,' he agreed, lighting another cigar, and not looking at her.

Caroline rose to her feet. 'I suppose I ought to be getting back. Miss Morgan will be wondering whether I've gone home.'

'Yes,' said Adam.

'Is that all?' she whispered, feeling the chill creeping over her again.

'Caro,' he groaned, 'what do you want me to say? I love you? God knows I do. I need you? That too. But I do not intend ruining your life, or alternatively allowing you to ruin mine.' He ran a hand through his short hair. 'Caro, if you ever did anything like that and we were married, I think I'd kill you! Now do you understand?'

'But, Adam—' she exclaimed.

'I'm busy,' he muttered, and turned away.

With a sob, Caroline ran to the door, wrenched it open, fled across Laura's domain and out of the door into the corridor. Once there, the tears would not be denied and she buried her face against the wall, sobbing achingly.

Caroline spent Christmas with Aunt Barbara in Hampstead. Aunt Barbara was a spinster and lived in a large house which stood in its own grounds. Caroline was very fond of her aunt, for she had always been kind to her and allowed her to do most of the things she had wanted to do. There had never been a lot of money, but that hadn't seemed to matter. They had been great friends and Caroline had learned all she knew about London from the old lady.

When she left to live with Amanda, Aunt Barbara acquired another elderly lady to come and be companion to her in exchange for a small salary. Her name was Miss Beale and she was in similar circumstances to Aunt Barbara except without any relatives at all. They shared the household duties and the situation worked out very well. They spent their time knitting and playing cards or dominoes and always welcomed Caroline when she visited them, bringing youth into the old house.

Caroline had never been made to feel guilty about leaving the ménage and she was grateful to be allowed to live her own life. After all, Aunt Barbara was in her seventies and was really her great-aunt, for she had been her father's aunt first of all, and she could have clung to Caroline in her twilight years. But Barbara's own youth had been marred by family ties and she had no intention of allowing Caroline to feel that she was a burden.

So Christmas passed quietly enough. Caroline by now had partly resigned herself to her parting from Adam, but whenever she saw his name in the paper or read anything concerning him, she felt the familiar longing sweep over her and she usually found herself in tears.

In mid-December his yacht *Circe* had sailed for the West Indies and she had felt his departure as painfully as though part of herself was being taken away from her. While he had been in London there had always been that chance that he might be in the lift in the mornings or alternatively she might meet him in the street. With his going there was no interest in anything any more.

And so by Christmas she felt completely drained of all emotion. She was able to laugh and joke with the two old ladies as though everything was fine, while her inner self seemed to sit apart and watch the proceedings with a cynical eye.

When she returned to the flat afterwards she tried to put all thoughts of Adam out of her mind. She became madly gay, going out with Amanda and her friends at every opportunity until Amanda got really worried about her. She realised Caroline was not giving herself time to think about her worries and so she refrained from saying anything.

The winter set in in earnest with heavy falls of snow, and the girls often had to walk to work because the buses were so late and so overcrowded. Caroline usually walked home too and found she enjoyed the unaccustomed exercise.

One evening when she left the Steinbeck Building it was very slippery underfoot and without warning she suddenly found herself on her back. She sat up, dusting the snow from her elbows, feeling quite ridiculous. A young man who was on his way to the Steinbeck Building grinned cheerfully and bending down helped her to her feet. She looked very lovely that evening, wrapped in her dark duffel coat, a scarlet hood almost hiding her silvery hair. With smiling eyes she turned to thank her helper and as she looked at the young man she started in amazement. 'John!' she exclaimed. 'I'm sorry I didn't recognise you.'

John Steinbeck thrust his hands into the pockets of his coat. 'Nor I you,' he answered, a smile playing round his mouth. Then with sudden concern, 'Are you all right? No bones broken?'

'I'm afraid not,' she replied provocatively.

John smiled. 'I guess I deserved that from the affair at Slayford,' he said easily. 'Gosh, that sounds like the title of some thriller!'

They both laughed and Caroline relaxed. John was very like Adam, and just being near him brought Adam nearer somehow. They were silent for a moment, looking at each other, and Caroline guessed John was wondering just what had been between herself and his father.

'Have you far to go?' he said at length, without any of the sarcasm he had displayed at their earlier meeting.

'To Gloucester Court, in Chelsea,' replied Caroline, brushing the last particles of snow from her coat.

'Would you care for a coffee?' he asked smilingly, looking down at her.

Caroline gasped. 'I'm sorry,' she said at last, 'but that was so unexpected. I thought I was the villain of the piece.'

John grinned. 'Well, will you come?'

'Yes. . .yes, please,' she agreed, and they began to walk along towards the coffee bar.

They turned into the newly-opened Pandora's Box and Caroline seated herself at one of the gaily coloured tables while John pushed his way to the counter. He came back with two steaming cups of coffee, plus a plate on which were two hamburgers and two Devonshire cream buns.

'I thought you might like a snack,' he said, as he seated himself opposite her. He was dressed in a light grey suit and a charcoal grey overcoat, his dark hair cut longer than his father's. Although it was the middle of January he looked brown and fit.

'Lovely,' said Caroline, smiling and accepting a hamburger. 'Are you on holiday?'

'Yes, until the beginning of February,' he nodded. 'Thank goodness! I've been studying for my exams and I'm enjoying the break.'

'Hm.' Caroline munched thoughtfully. 'Didn't... didn't you want to go with your father?' she asked, forcing her voice to sound coolly interested.

John nodded. 'I've just got back,' he replied, looking across at her with his clear blue eyes. 'I was on the yacht for a month. But I came back earlier than necessary to acclimatise myself before returning to college.'

'Oh, I see.' Caroline suddenly lost her appetite. The casual way he mentioned his sojourn on the *Circe* was bringing back memories vividly to her mind.

'Yes, it was great getting away from all this and spending a few weeks in the sun.'

'Did you go alone?' she asked suddenly, remembering Toni Landon and the way she had looked at Adam.

'Yes, just me,' he nodded lazily. 'I only wish it was still ahead of me.'

Caroline sighed. 'You're very lucky,' she commented, not thinking of the yacht or the sun, only of Adam.

John looked down at his coffee. 'Is everything over between you and Dad?'

'As far as he's concerned,' she replied huskily.

'And you?'

'I'd rather not talk about it.'

'Okay. Say, how would you like to take in a movie before I buy you some supper?'

Caroline stared at him. 'Are you serious?' she exclaimed.

'Never more serious in my life,' he replied, smiling. 'I was interested in you from the moment I first saw you. And you knew it, didn't you?'

'But what about Toni?' she asked, frowning.

'Hell, that was over ages ago. You don't know me very well or you wouldn't ask questions like that.'

'All right, thank you.'

They discussed the merits of different films and finally decided on a French film with English subtitles. They came out roaring with laughter at the inadequacy of the subtitles and Caroline found she was enjoying herself much more than she had done for ages.

They had supper at a French restaurant just to round the evening off and ate frogs' legs to be completely cosmopolitan. They drank real continental-flavoured coffee and Caroline heaved a sigh of contentment when it was over.

'That was fabulous,' she breathed, drawing on her cigarette. 'I have enjoyed myself, John. Thank you.'

'It's been my pleasure,' he replied easily. 'When do I see you again?'

Caroline studied the glowing tip of the cigarette. 'Are you sure you want to?' she asked quietly.

'Sure I'm sure,' he answered, leaning towards her across the table. 'I always knew my father had good taste.'

Caroline flushed scarlet and drew back. John inwardly cursed himself for his stupidity and apologised. 'I'm awfully sorry,' he said. 'I didn't mean to sound patronising.'

Caroline shrugged. 'It's all right,' she said quietly. 'Shall we go?'

They took a taxi to Gloucester Court and in the taxi John was still apologetic.

'Look,' he said eagerly, 'my car is at Slayford, how about letting me pick you up tomorrow evening and we'll have dinner? Not at Slayford,' he continued hastily when she stared at him. 'At some restaurant, hm?'

Sure she was being all kinds of a fool, Caroline reluctantly agreed, and John was thankful. She was a charming girl and he urgently wanted to see her again.

The following evening John called for Caroline in his low red sports car at seven o'clock. Amanda, who saw the sports car arrive and only knew of John as a boy whom Caroline had accidentally met the previous day, whistled appreciatively as she turned away from the window.

'How do you do it, Caroline?' she exclaimed with a wry grin. 'You seem to attract the most attractive men, and all with big bank balances. Can't you introduce me to some of them?'

'Lots of boys drive sports cars,' Caroline exclaimed easily. She had no wish to make Amanda suspicious.

'But none of the same calibre as the one that has just arrived,' remarked Amanda, flinging herself into a chair. 'I expect Daddy bought it for him for his birthday or something.'

Caroline's face whitened suddenly and Amanda frowned. 'Are you all right, honey?' she asked quickly. 'Because if you're not I'm quite willing to go down there and offer to take your place.'

Caroline had to smile. 'Yes, I'm all right,' she

exclaimed, a shade too brightly. The nausea she felt at the mention of John's father would not be denied. Would she ever be able to hear his name without feeling in a state of collapse?

She was wearing a green trouser suit, and John was wholly appreciative, and his eyes were openly admiring when she removed her coat in the foyer of the restaurant he had taken her to.

The waiter apparently knew John, for he showed them to a secluded alcove where a table for two was set between low velvet couches.

John ordered the meal, and then offered Caroline a cigarette while they waited for it to be served.

'Tell me,' he said, 'how did you come to meet my father?'

Caroline ran a tongue over her suddenly dry lips. She had expected this question and so she ought to be prepared for it. 'I work in the Steinbeck Building,' she replied quietly. 'I'm a shorthand-typist in the typing pool.'

'I see,' John nodded, apparently satisfied with this explanation. She did not have the ignominy of explaining about the lift. 'I'm sorry if I seem to harp on the subject, but having no mother, and being an only child, I tend to be rather possessive about my father.'

Caroline nodded, looking sympathetically at him. She could understand this. He seemed so much younger than herself, if not in age then in manner. She could even understand his resentment displayed at Slayford as it must have been a great shock, sprung upon him suddenly like that, without warning. She wondered now, as he spoke, whether he was really aware of what the situation had been between herself and Adam. Perhaps if he only thought of them as friends it was all to the good. He obviously had changed his early low opinion of her.

Changing the subject, she said: 'Tell me about the West Indies. Did you have an exciting time?'

John sighed, relaxed again. 'Yes, marvellous,' he replied, nodding. 'My father owns a house in Jamaica that stands almost on the beach. It's a private strip of beach, of course, and the sand is really quite white. The sea is very warm and very blue.'

'It sounds wonderful,' commented Caroline, smiling. 'And you're very tanned. Did you bathe a lot?'

'At least once every day,' said John, smiling reminiscently. 'We spent most of our time in swimming trunks and sweaters.'

Caroline could imagine this. How wonderful it would have been to spend a holiday with Adam! To see him all day and every day. It was a dream, which had little hope of becoming a fact.

The meal John had ordered was delicious and afterwards they went on to a club in Chelsea where most of the members were teenagers and nothing more intoxicating than Coca-Cola was sold.

He drove her home at eleven-thirty and stopped outside the flats, turning towards her with a smile.

'Well,' he said, 'did you enjoy youself, and if so, will you repeat the experience?'

Caroline's eyes twinkled. 'Of course I enjoyed myself,' she replied, 'and I would like to see you again.'

'Good.' John leant on the steering wheel. 'How about going to a show tomorrow, if I can get tickets?'

Caroline bent her head. 'What sort of show?' she

asked, remembering the last show she had seen and who she had been with.

'Anything you like. By the way, what do you like? Lowbrow or highbrow stuff? I know very little about you.'

'Well, I like concerts,' confessed Caroline candidly, 'but I like some pop music. It depends how I feel.'

'Right. That's okay by me. Do you want to go somewhere like the Festival Hall tomorrow night?'

Caroline's eyes lit up. 'Oh, yes, please. They're doing Grieg's Piano Concerto, and I adore that.'

'Good. We'll do that, then.'

In the days that followed John took Caroline out almost every night, giving her no time to think at all. They attended concerts and went to a new musical extravaganza, usually following them by supper at a restaurant. They even went to a party given by some fellow students from the university and Caroline thoroughly enjoyed herself. John never tried to be more than friendly with her and she was glad. There were no complications to concern herself with.

John rarely discussed his father, although when he did talk about Adam, Caroline found she was unconscionably interested. John was clearly proud of his father and told Caroline more about the woman who had been his mother.

'She wasn't at all like Dad,' he said, sighing as he remembered those times. They were sitting in a coffee bar after spending the evening at Covent Garden. 'She was really quite contented to stay in the same old rut year after year. I don't think she cared whether Dad was successful or not and she certainly gave him no encouragement. They were so different, you see. I can't imagine what attracted them to one another.'

Caroline shrugged. She was remembering what Adam had told her.

'In a way, I think it was as well that she died when she did,' continued John slowly. 'Oh, I know that sounds a horrible thing to say, but she would never have been happy the way things turned out.'

Caroline nodded. 'There are women like that, I suppose,' she said quietly. 'Have there been many women in your father's life since then?'

She was dreading his answer, but when it came she was glad.

'Caroline, my father is a millionaire. Even if he looked like Frankenstein's monster there would always be women, of some sort. To some women, money paints masks over the ugliest faces. And of course, as Dad is very attractive, for his age, there have been plenty.'

'Oh!' Turning the knife in the wound, she said: 'I suppose it's understandable. Money means everything to many people.'

'Yes.' John looked reflective. 'However, if on the other hand, you were to ask whether he had had any serious affairs, I could honestly say "No." I really don't believe that there's a woman alive today for whom he would give up his freedom.'

Perhaps he was right, she thought, sighing. Maybe he had seized on the excuse of her youth to let himself out of an awkward situation. After all, she had behaved with abandon that day at Slayford. Perhaps he thought she was cheap. With these torturing thoughts drifting round in her head, Caroline was sure she would have no sleep that night.

John returned to the university during the first week in February and began writing to her almost at once. He wrote regularly, every couple of days, although Caroline only replied weekly. He had not contacted his father to tell him he was meeting Caroline at her request, but soon after he left London, Adam returned.

He flew into London Airport and there was a picture of him in the *Morning Gazette*. Caroline read the caption on her way to work and wondered idly whether she would see him about the office building. She doubted it as she was usually early for work now, and besides, she would hate to have him think she was being deliberately late simply to see him.

Things had settled down in the typing pool now. Ruth had naturally assumed that nothing had come of her meeting with Adam Steinbeck and Caroline did not disillusion her. The fewer people who knew of that disastrous affair the better. No one, not even Amanda, knew she was going out with Adam Steinbeck's son, and she supposed that she was courting notoriety in that direction also if anyone was to find out.

At the beginning of March, John came home to Slayford for a long weekend and met Caroline for a meal on his first night. His earlier suntan had died away and he looked tired, as though he had been studying half the night.

'Won't your father wonder where you are?' asked Caroline as they sat trying to eat rice with chopsticks in a Chinese restaurant.

'Not tonight,' replied John, smiling. 'He's giving a dinner party at Slayford for the directors of the Corporation and their wives. They always have a get-together once a year when the yearly statements are published.

It's a sort of celebration of the profits they've made.'
He sounded disparaging. 'I wouldn't want to be there,
and of course, he knows it. He usually lets me off.'

'But aren't you interested?' exclaimed Caroline.
'After all, you'll inherit the whole affair some day.'

'Me?' John looked astounded. 'Can you see me in
big business? Oh, no. That's not my line. I intend to
have a career quite apart from the Steinbeck Corporation. I don't want to spend my days locked up in a
stuffy office. Life's got more to it than that.'

Caroline sighed. 'Well, what will happen then?' she
asked, interested in spite of herself.

'Well, unless the old man marries again, and pro-
duces another son, I guess one of my cousins in Boston,
Massachusetts, USA will find themselves pretty rich
one of these fine days. This last he spoke with a pro-
nounced American accent and Caroline laughed
helplessly.

'All right,' she said at last, 'so how is Ad. . .your
father?'

'Okay, I guess. He's looking a bit tired but otherwise
he's fit.' He grimaced down at his plate. 'I'll never
get this stuff in my mouth. I give in, let's have some
spoons.'

John was home from Thursday until the following
Tuesday morning and Caroline saw him for some time
each day. On Saturday it was her birthday and they
went to Brighton and spent the whole day there. John
had found out the date of her birthday earlier in their
acquaintanceship and when he called for her on
Saturday morning he indicated a small package on the
parcel shelf of the car.

Eagerly, before starting the car, he urged her to open

it and laughing, she complied. Then the laughter died
in her throat when she opened the jeweller's box that
had emerged from the wrapping paper and found herself looking at the platinum bracelet whose emeralds,
rubies and diamonds winked mockingly at her.

Her first impulse was to thrust it back at him in
horror, but as she lifted it with trembling fingers she
realised what a ridiculous gesture that would be. He
would not understand the significance of it. She would
only hurt his feelings, and she did not want to do that.
It was ironic, she thought achingly, that Adam should
have given the bracelet to his son to give to one of
his girl-friends and that particular girl-friend should
happen to be herself.

She suddenly became aware that John was looking
at her face in consternation. 'What's wrong?' he asked,
puzzled. 'Don't you like it? I was sure you would.'

'Oh, John,' she began slowly, 'it's beautiful. But I
couldn't possibly accept such a costly present from
you, really.'

'Is that all?' John looked relieved and smiled. 'Don't
be silly. I shall be offended if you refuse. Please,
Caroline. I want you to have it, to wear it.'

Caroline sighed. It seemed that fate intended that
she should have the bracelet, but she felt she hated the
brilliant thing. It would be a continual reminder of
things that might have been and Adam's rejection
of her.

'Very well,' she said at last. 'Thank you, John. I
can honestly say I've never seen or owned such a
beautiful piece of jewellery.'

John looked and felt pleased with himself.

'Good,' he said. 'Now, I'm going to give you a

really wonderful day. A day to remember.'

And so he did. Had it not been for the constant reminders of Adam in his manner and attitudes, Caroline thought it would have been the most perfect birthday she had ever spent.

They returned to London in the evening and went to a nightclub to celebrate her entry into the 'drinking classes' as he put it.

The following day, Sunday, John could only meet her in the late evening. He had spent the day with his father at Slayford and had had difficulty in explaining why he hadn't brought his current girl-friend to meet his father. Adam was used to John's conquests being exhibited before him and could not understand his son's rather strained conversation concerning the girl he was going to meet that evening. However, he did not probe too deeply, relying on John to tell him if he wanted to.

John told Caroline a little of this and Caroline felt awful.

'I expect you'll have to tell him,' she said, sighing. 'I don't want to cause dissension between you.'

'I will, some time,' said John, sensing her discomfiture. 'Don't worry. He won't object.'

Caroline wondered about this. Would he object? And if he didn't what would it prove?

They spent the rest of the evening at a jazz club in a cellar in Chelsea. The music was played by a black band and it was wild and pulsating. At John's suggestion Caroline was dressed in scarlet velvet lounging pants and a black sweater and was glad she had taken his advice. All the members seemed to dress in this way and danced with abandon to the African rhythm.

After a particularly energetic session, Caroline collapsed against John in one corner of the big room.

'You're very good,' she confessed breathlessly, 'but I'm exhausted.'

'You're not so bad yourself,' he replied, looking down at her as she tried to straighten up, away from him. She was quite unconscious of the effect she was having on John, his senses roused by the passionate music.

Suddenly, he bent his head and she felt his mouth against the side of her neck, his body trembling against hers.

'Oh, John!' She drew away, breathing quickly.

'Am I blacklisted?' he muttered, running a hand through his tousled hair.

'No, of course not,' she answered, not quite aware of how to handle this situation. She had not considered this happening somehow, although she was aware that John had been watching her of late with more than friendship in his eyes. She had hoped against hope that she was no more to him than he was to her, but apparently this was not so. They had had a lot of fun and lots of laughs, but that was as far as she wanted it to go. She could never love anyone else in the way she loved Adam and she knew instinctively that that was the right way. No matter what happened, John could never be more than second-best.

'Surely you'd guessed how I felt?' he asked her, studying her face in the semi-darkness of the quiet alcove.

'No, I'm afraid I didn't,' she replied restlessly. 'Oh, John, what can I say. . .'

He shrugged. 'Please, don't say anything. Forget it.

It was too much to hope you might be feeling the same way.'

Caroline sighed, shaking her head. 'Does this mean we stop seeing each other?' she asked.

'No. At least I hope not,' he protested, grasping her shoulders. 'Caroline, I'm in love with you. I've never felt this way before. I must go on seeing you.'

Caroline hesitated and then moved closer to him. 'Kiss me, John. If you want to?'

John needed no second bidding and bent his head to hers. His mouth was warm and tender and very pleasant, but as they kissed Caroline found herself imagining it was Adam kissing her and her response intoxicated John. The kiss hardened in its passion and with a stifled cry she drew back, rubbing a hand across her lips. It was hateful making use of John in this way.

When they drove home later, Caroline felt undecided and said:

'Are you really sure you want to go on seeing me?'

'Of course,' he replied swiftly. 'Who knows, one day you might suddenly find yourself in love with me. I can only hope, and I want to be around if that happens. After all, you seemed attracted to my father. Am I so different?'

'No. You're very like him,' answered Caroline.

'Good. Then that's settled,' he said, with a smile, and she relaxed.

After John had returned to Radbury, Caroline found herself more alone than ever somehow. Whether their closer relationship had anything to do with it, she wasn't sure, but she certainly missed him.

However, she began to take a more conscientious interest in her work and Miss Morgan found she was the most efficient in the typing pool. In the Steinbeck Corporation typing pool, good workers were always appreciated and so when one of the senior secretaries left Caroline was offered her position. She accepted with alacrity, although she was aware that her promotion was considered favouritism by the other girls. The old story about herself and Adam was brought up and Caroline was glad when she moved into her new office.

She was to be private secretary to Mr Lawson, who was in charge of salaries. His staff calculated income tax and insurance contributions together with all the other work connected with wages. Caroline's work proved much more varied and interesting and she enjoyed working without supervision.

As Easter neared, Caroline found herself looking forward to John's vacation. In one letter he had told her that his father was flying to America in May to see John's grandmother and wanted John to accompany him. John said that he was trying to get out of it and as yet nothing was decided.

One afternoon in early April, Caroline's boss did not return from his lunch and at two o'clock his wife rang to say that he had developed a severe migraine and was taking the afternoon off. Caroline said how sorry she was before Mrs Lawson rang off and then busied herself with a pile-up of overdue filing. She occupied an office of her own and was working industriously when the telephone pealed beside her. It was the internal telephone and expecting to speak to one of the office staff Caroline lifted the receiver.

'Mr Lawson's office. Miss Sinclair speaking,' she said easily.

There was a moment's silence and then a husky male voice asked quietly: 'Caroline. Is that you?'

Caroline's legs went weak and she sank down on to the edge of the desk.

'Adam,' she breathed, and then with a semblance of pride she asked: 'What can I do for you?'

'I wanted to speak to Mr Lawson,' replied Adam, still in that quiet, assured voice. 'I didn't know you worked for him.'

'I'm Mr Lawson's secretary,' replied Caroline stiffly. She had realised that he had been as surprised as herself when they spoke. After all, had he wanted to get in touch with her he would hardly have done so at the office. She swallowed hard.

'Mr Lawson isn't in this afternoon. His wife rang to say he had a severe attack of migraine and was going straight to bed.'

'I see.' He sighed. 'Never mind. I'll contact him later in the week.'

There was silence for a minute and then he said: 'How are you?'

'I'm fine,' she replied, forcing her voice to sound light and disinterested. 'And you? Did you enjoy your holiday?'

'My holiday?. . .oh. . .you mean in January. Yes, it was very pleasant. John came with me for a few weeks during his Christmas vacation. Did you have a good Christmas?'

'Fairly good,' agreed Caroline lightly. This small talk between them was so frustrating. Why didn't he ring off?'

'Tell me,' he said, suddenly intense, 'who is this young man you're going around with?'

Caroline was astounded. How on earth did he know she was going out with anybody? Was he having her investigated or something? Suddenly she felt angry. How dare he ask her such a question? It was nothing to him but idle curiosity.

'I can't imagine what business it is of yours,' she exclaimed furiously. 'Where on earth do you get your information?'

'Don't get so angry,' he said easily. 'I'm not having you followed, if that's what you think. I simply happened to see you having a meal in a coffee bar in Chelsea a few weeks ago with a young man. Is it Davison?'

'No, it's not. Didn't you see him for yourself?' Her anger had subsided somewhat.

'No, I'm afraid not.'

'I see. Well, his name is John Steinbeck,' she replied coolly, wanting to hurt him as he had hurt her. Besides, John had always wanted to tell his father and make their association open.

She heard Adam's sharp intake of breath and then he snapped:

'Are you joking, Caroline?'

'Why should I joke about a thing like that?' she asked, almost hating herself now for being so brutal about it. What must he be thinking of her? If only she could see his face. Just to see if he cared. Suddenly the telephone went dead and she realised he had hung up on her. With a sigh she replaced her receiver on the cradle and shivered uncontrollably. That was that, with a vengeance! And what would happen now? She lit a cigarette and drew on it thankfully.

She did not have to wait long to find out. It was

only minutes before the door of her office was flung
open and Adam strode into the room, closing the door
decisively behind him. His broad frame made the room
seem suddenly tiny and nervously she rose to her feet,
conscious of the fact that her hair needed combing and
her nose was probably shining.

He looked big and just as attractive as ever, although
he definitely looked tired, as though he was
sleeping badly.

'Well,' she murmured shakily, 'what a surprise!'

Adam frowned, looking down at her through his
thick lashes.

'Did you honestly think you could tell me a thing
like that without my turning a hair?' he snapped
angrily. 'God, Caro, are you trying to drive me out of
my mind?'

Caroline flushed and sank down on to the
desk again.

'Of course not,' she answered quickly. 'It's simply
that I met John by accident in January while you were
away and since then we've been meeting each other
whenever he's in town.'

'As simple as that,' he said cynically, lighting a
cigar with impatient fingers. 'Thank God I wasn't foolish enough to believe in your protestations of sincerity.
Here we are, only four months later, and you've quite
forgotten, haven't you?'

Caroline stubbed out her cigarette. 'How dare you
preach to me!' she cried angrily. 'Of course I haven't
forgotten anything. My feelings for you will never
change. But as you don't intend to do anything about
it, I feel I'm at liberty to do as I please.'

'My own son,' he muttered bitterly. 'John, of all

people. Why? To take revenge?'

'No, of course not. Hasn't it occurred to you that I might enjoy John's company simply because he is your son?'

Adam turned away and crossed to the window, looking out without really seeing the view.

'All right,' he said heavily. 'I know I have no right to interfere. I apologise.'

Caroline clenched her fists. Her whole being yearned to go to him, to comfort him, to assure him that he need have no qualms about John taking his place. But her pride would not let her do it. After all, she was not even now completely sure of his meaning in all this and he had chosen to ignore his need of her in the past. If he truly believed she would be happier with a younger man then perhaps indeed John might be that man. After all, he loved her. She forced herself to stay where she was.

'You're looking tired,' she said at last. 'Are you sleeping?'

'Thank you, yes,' he replied, coldly, and turning he looked at her. His gaze was brooding and intense, a grimness about his mouth. 'I expect it's old age. I was thirty-nine last month.'

'And I was eighteen,' she replied quietly.

'I'm afraid I forgot your birthday,' he said with a shrug of his broad shoulders.

'Your son remembered,' remarked Caroline, and then with feeling, 'I was given a platinum bracelet.'

Adam's eyebrows ascended. 'Indeed? So you got it in the end?'

She flushed. 'Not in quite the expected circumstances,' she said coldly. She felt the old ache in her stomach at the remembrance of it all. 'And not through choice, believe me, but John wouldn't have understood, would he?'

Adam whitened visibly, then he walked to the door, slowly.

'I don't think there's anything more to be said,' he muttered wearily. 'Goodbye, Caroline.'

'Goodbye. . . Mr Steinbeck.' Caroline refused to look up as he went out closing the door behind him. Then as the door clicked, she buried her face in her hands.

CHAPTER SIX

SHE wrote and told John that Adam had found out about their friendship and was relieved when he wrote back saying that his father had already telephoned him about it. John's letter said that Adam had been non-committal about the whole affair, but that that was only to be expected in the rather strange circumstances. Caroline realised tht this was so and was glad that Adam had not vetoed their association as he could so easily have done. Did this mean he didn't care any more? After all, he dictated John's income and paid his university fees and he could have made him dance to any tune he cared to play. However, as she thought about it Caroline came to the conclusion that Adam probably had decided it was nothing to do with him, in his implacable and stubborn way, and therefore intended to do nothing about it. She herself had come up against this wall of reserve in him before and she only prayed that one day she might have the chance to bridge it by explaining all that the evening with Mark Davison had meant.

In a later letter from John, he told her that Adam no longer pressed him to accompany him to America in May and he wondered whether Caroline could take a week's holiday during his Easter vacation and spend a week with him in Paris.

Caroline felt quite excited at the prospect of a trip to France and as her holiday could be taken at any time she decided to go with him. She wrote back agreeing to his suggestion with fervour. It would be just the thing to take her out of herself. John's reply to her acceptance was flatteringly jubilant and he wrote saying that he would make all the arrangements if she could get herself a passport.

Amanda, who was still unaware of John's identity, was not so keen on the idea and advised Caroline to think carefully before embarking on such a dangerous trip. After all, Amanda reasoned, she knew hardly anything about the boy and had never met his parents.

However, Caroline managed to sidetrack her most pertinent questions and evaded giving a direct answer to his identity. She didn't quite know why she was doing this. She simply didn't want another lecture.

And then, a week before the start of John's vacation, Caroline received a telephone call which was to change her whole life. The call was from Miss Beale, advising her that her Aunt Barbara had suffered a severe heart attack that morning and had never regained consciousness.

Caroline was shocked to the core of her being. Aunt Barbara had been her only living relative and her death severed all her connections with the past. It was shattering to realise that she was completely alone in the world. Aunt Barbara had always been there to turn to if need be, the necessary root that everyone likes to feel can be relied upon. Now there was only emptiness.

It was a hollow-eyed Caroline who attended the funeral at the little church near her aunt's house and who stood, dressed in a dark suit and coat, as the coffin was lowered into the grave. Her aunt had looked so small when she had seen her lying in her bed that dreadful morning she died, and now, seeing the coffin for the last time, Caroline felt the tears scalding her cheeks.

Mr Manson, her aunt's solicitor, who had dealt with her aunt's affairs for years, was very sympathetic and after her aunt's few friends had departed from the old house, he asked Caroline and Miss Beale to join him in the library.

As she followed Miss Beale into the book-lined room Caroline looked about her regretfully. She had spent many happy hours as a child amongst these old volumes and it had been her aunt who had taught her to appreciate the good music which she now enjoyed so much. Fourteen years of her life had been spent within this old building and she knew that without Aunt Barbara the place would never be the same again. Although quite old when Caroline came to her, orphaned and alone, she had always been young in heart and had always made her young charge feel wanted and loved.

When they were all seated at the old desk which occupied the centre of the room, Mr Manson drew out an envelope from his briefcase and said:

'Your aunt's last will and testament, Miss Sinclair.'

Caroline looked surprised. As far as she knew her aunt only owned this house and she had never presumed that she herself would ever possess it.

Mr Manson placed his rimless glasses on his rather angular nose and began to read its contents. The earlier part of the will dealt with some donations to charities which Caroline's aunt had favoured, and Caroline was quite astonished that her aunt, who had always lived so frugally, had amassed sufficient funds to allow her to leave such generous amounts.

Then came a gift of five hundred pounds to Miss Beale, who flushed in surprise and said: 'How very kind, when I had only known her such a short time,' in her shy little voice.

Finally, Mr Manson turned to Caroline.

'The remainder of the estate, including this house which you may sell if you so desire, is left to you, Miss Sinclair. After death duties, etc., I estimate you should have some twenty-five thousand pounds, plus of course the price you get for this house if you decide to sell.'

Caroline gasped and lay back in her chair, absolutely astounded. 'Twenty-five thousand pounds!' she exclaimed shakily. 'But, Mr Manson, my aunt had very little money.'

In the last few years your aunt has been dabbling on the Stock Exchange,' he replied calmly. 'She had a very good broker and has been extremely clever. She was always a keen business woman, although when she was your age she had no opportunity to show her prowess. She was always careful with money and her gambles paid off.'

Caroline lit a cigarette with trembling fingers. She still couldn't take it in. She was rich! She had independent means!

'I had no idea,' she exclaimed, shaking her head. 'Oh, Mr Manson, what can I say?'

'I suggest you say nothing,' he replied with a little smile. 'Miss Sinclair was nearly eighty. She had had a long life and I suspect she would be glad that her end came so swiftly and that she was no burden to anybody. She wanted you to have the money to do the things that she never had the chance to do. She told me many times that you reminded her of herself when she was young, although of course, in those days young girls did not leave home and have their own flats in London. Nor did she have the chance to run around with young men as girls do nowadays. Take the money and enjoy it as she intended you to do. However, if I might make a suggestion, don't advertise the fact too blatantly that you are now a rich young woman. Fortune-hunters are all to plentiful, I'm afraid.'

Caroline sighed. 'Thank you. I'd like you to continue as my solicitor if you would. Then any problems I encounter can be talked over with you.'

'Very well, Miss Sinclair. I should be always ready to offer any advice if necessary. And now I'll leave you. I think it would be as well if you came into my office tomorrow morning and we will discuss the details and your immediate plans. Right?'

'Yes, of course. And thank you. I'm very grateful for all you've done.'

'Not at all,' he answered with a smile. 'It's my job, you know. And now, if you ladies will excuse me. . .?'

After he had gone, and Miss Beale had gone upstairs to pack her things, Caroline sat for a long time staring into the fire. It was so unbelievable. Suddenly she was a woman of means. Free from all ties. She could give up her job, go anywhere she liked, the world was amazingly her oyster.

Free. The word seemed to mock her. Even now, with all the sadness of Aunt Barbara's death, the sudden shock of finding herself in this enviable position, the love she bore for Adam Steinbeck wove its own fetters about her. She would never be free of loving

Adam and she might as well admit it. She still wanted him just as much. Although she now had the chance to go anywhere that took her fancy, she found the thought of leaving Adam in England tortured her. How could she go thousands of miles away from him? How could she?

But with an effort she dragged herself back to the present. She felt so alone, and she felt she must know someone who cared about her. Then, like a drowning man seizes at a straw Caroline remembered John, and with a swift burst of energy she rose and went out into the hall where the telephone was installed. She rang his rooms in Radbury and miraculously he was in and answered her ring.

'Caroline!' he exclaimed, his voice warm with pleasure. 'I'm so glad you've rung. I got your letter this morning telling me about your aunt. I'm very sorry. Please accept my condolences.'

'Thank you, John. Oh, it's lovely to hear your voice.' Truthfully, his obvious pleasure at hearing from her had warmed her heart, and she really sounded thrilled to speak to him.

'Hey,' John's voice was teasing, 'don't use that tone on the telephone. Save it for when I'm home with you. I've never known you so enthusiastic with me.'

'Oh, John,' she exclaimed with a sigh, 'I was sitting here feeling thoroughly dejected and miserable and suddenly I thought of you. I picked up the phone and there you are. It's wonderful!'

'I see. Well, honey, is it all over?'

'Yes, it's over. But I've a surprise for you. I am now the inheritor of this house and twenty-five thousand pounds.'

'What?' John was as astounded as she had been.

'Yes. I was dumbfounded. Poor Aunt Barbara. It certainly was a closely guarded secret and she didn't use any of the money to make her own life easier. Only her solicitor knew she was gambling on the stock market.'

'Amazing!' John dispelled his breath in a low whistle. 'So now you're an heiress. At least no one can now accuse you of wanting my money.' He chuckled. 'Seriously though, Caro, are you all right? You sound rather het up and nervous. You're not going back to work now, are you?'

'Not tomorrow at least,' she replied. 'I'm going to see the solicitor in the morning. I'm staying here tonight with Miss Beale, she was Aunt Barbara's companion, and then we'll both be leaving. I'm going to put the house up for sale. It's a great barn of a place, and besides, I don't need a house, not just for myself. I'll arrange that with Mr Manson tomorrow.'

'And our week in Paris? Is that to be postponed?'

Caroline sighed. 'I don't know, John. When do you come back home?'

'I suppose I could come tomorrow,' he replied slowly. 'I've very little to clear up. Why?'

Caroline shivered involuntarily. 'Do come back tomorrow,' she murmured, so softly that he could just hear, 'I need you, John. We'll decide about Paris then.'

'Will do,' answered John in return. 'When you speak to me like that, you know I'd do anything.'

After they had rung off, Caroline mounted the stairs to her room, and looked around sadly. No longer would she be coming here for holidays, or for Christmas. No more Saturday visits from Aunt Barbara at the flat.

She felt as though one phase of her life had ended and another was just beginning. As she sat on her bed she wondered whether she had been right in telling John that she needed him. Wouldn't she have been more truthful if she had said that she needed Adam and if she could not have him then any man might fill the gap?

Amanda was astonished and pleased at Caroline's unexpected inheritance. On the few occasions she had met Caroline's aunt, she had thought her a rather pleasant old lady, but certainly no gambler. Aunt Barbara's rather shabby attire and undemanding manner had really hidden the true Barbara Sinclair.

Caroline was amused by her shocked countenance, which turned to amazement when Caroline told her she intended to pay five hundred pounds into Amanda's bank account.

Amanda spread wide her hands. 'Honestly, Caroline, are you sure? I mean, that's an awful lot of money to ge giving away.'

'Why not?' exclaimed Caroline with a sigh. 'I want to do this for you and goodness knows I can afford it.'

'What can I say?' cried Amanda, hugging her impulsively.

'I'm glad you're pleased,' replied Caroline, hugging Amanda in return. 'We've been such good friends, Amanda, and I'd like to think of you with something to fall back upon. I'd also like us to find another flat which we can share. I don't want us to lose touch with one another as we will if I leave here. I don't know what I'm going to do yet. I'm going to resign from Steinbecks, of course, and have a holiday somewhere, and then...who knows? I may find myself another secretarial post. I can't imagine myself being continually idle. I would have no point in my life if I had nothing to do.'

'But, Caroline, you can go on a world tour...anything of that kind. Surely you want to visit other lands, meet other kinds of people?'

'I don't know.' Caroline shrugged her slim shoulders helplessly.

Intuitively, Amanda said: 'Caroline, you're not still hankering after that man?'

They both knew which man she meant.

Caroline forced a smile. 'I must get changed. John's coming home from university today and he's calling for me at six.'

Amanda frowned. She was well aware of Caroline's nervous disposition. With a determined stiffening of her shoulders she said:

'Caroline, you haven't answered my question.'

'No. So I haven't,' remarked Caroline shortly, and walked away into the bedroom.

While Caroline was washing at the basin Amanda lit a cigarette and paced restlessly round the living-room and then she walked to the door of the bedroom. She was worried about Caroline. It was obvious that her inheritance meant less than nothing to her compared with something else, Adam Steinbeck.

'Tell me,' Amanda said suddenly, 'this "John" you're going out with; who is he? What does he do?'

'I told you, he's at Radbury University,' replied Caroline, wriggling into a slim-fitting jersey dress of a creamy colour which toned with her skin and silvery hair.

'I know you did,' persisted Amanda. 'But where does he come from? What's his surname? What do his parents do?'

'Such a lot of questions,' exclaimed Caroline lightly, but a hot flush stained her cheeks, belying her attempt at banter. 'His mother is dead.'

Amanda suddenly felt something go click inside her. All the little things that Caroline had merely hinted at during the past few months fell into place. Her failure to tell Amanda his surname; their chance meeting when Caroline had never done such a thing before; the expensive sports car; the visit to Paris; and finally his mother being dead.

'Is his name Steinbeck, by any chance?' said Amanda.

Caroline swung round, her hairbrush in her hand, and her face gave Amanda her answer.

'Yes,' she said with a sigh. 'I'm quite glad you know at last. I've wanted to tell you often enough, goodness knows.'

Amanda shook her head in a bewildered fashion. 'What are you playing at, Caroline?' she cried. 'Is this some obscure way of playing off his father? Or are you genuinely interested in him? In view of your reactions to Adam Steinbeck's name I should say the former is probably the case.'

Caroline shivered. 'It's not really either of your conclusions,' she explained, brushing her hair slowly. 'I like John, I'm not having revenge on Adam, but I don't really understand myself why I'm going out with him.'

Amanda snorted angrily, 'Caroline, are you making use of this boy? Pretending he's Adam, simply because he's that man's son?'

'No.' The word was torn from Caroline, and bright tears sparkled in her eyes. 'I really do like him, Amanda. He's kind and sweet. . .and oh, God, I've got to have somebody.'

Amanda sighed heavily. Caroline was too strung up to care what she said. 'And John,' she continued relentlessly. 'Does he just *like* you?'

'No.' Caroline replaced the hairbrush on the dressing table. 'He says he's in love with me.'

'I thought as much,' sighed Amanda. 'Caroline, can't you see, you're only hurting yourself more by persisting with this. Find yourself a new boy-friend. One who has no connections with the Steinbeck family. Now you've got the money you can meet all kinds of people.'

'No.' Caroline was adamant. 'As long as John is satisfied, I'm all right.'

Amanda flung the end of her cigarette into the hearth. 'And what's to be the outcome? Has he asked you to marry him?'

'Not yet.'

'But he will, no doubt,' groaned Amanda. 'And what will you say? Yes?'

Caroline applied a coral lipstick to her mouth. 'I might,' she shrugged, voicing for the first time a thought which had been on her mind for some time. 'After all, I don't want to become an old maid.'

Amanda looked aghast. 'Caroline Sinclair! You're only eighteen years of age. That sort of comment is downright ridiculous and you know it.'

'Oh, all right, Amanda. Don't go on,' exclaimed Caroline with feeling.

'But I must,' exclaimed Amanda. 'Don't you see?

You're letting this infatuation for Adam Steinbeck drive you to doing things you wouldn't normally contemplate.'

'It's not infatuation,' cried Caroline angrily.

'Very well. But you've just become an heiress. Don't throw your life away now. You've everything to live for. Every dream you've ever had can come true.'

'Except one,' said Caroline harshly. 'Amanda, I love Adam. I will never love anyone else and it's driving me crazy. Can't you see?' She twisted her hands. 'Nothing has any meaning without him. I need him, Amanda, but he just doesn't want to know.' She bit her lip. 'And so I have John. At least part of John is Adam. He can talk about him and I enjoy his company. Why is it wrong to do that?'

'Because you're torturing yourself,' cried Amanda. 'Caroline, we've been like sisters. Please, give this boy up. Give yourself a chance to forget them both. Go away.'

'No.' Caroline shook her head. 'I'm afraid I'm too much of a coward to do that.'

Suddenly a horn sounded in the mews below. Caroline hurried through to look out of the window, pulling on her red coat.

'It's John,' she said. 'I've got to go, Mandy.'

Amanda sighed. 'All right. See you later.'

Caroline hurried down the stairs, pushing the last few minutes out of her mind. Her conversation with Amanda was over. What she had said had to be. She needed John, and it was good to know he loved her.

She reached the entrance to the flats just as John was coming in and they almost collided with one another.

'Caro,' he exclaimed softly, surveying her flushed

cheeks. 'Oh, come here. . .' and he pulled her to him, his mouth seeking hers.

She clung to him momentarily and then released herself breathlessly.

'Hello, John,' she whispered. 'It's good to see you again.'

'Likewise, I'm sure,' he grinned down at her. 'You must have missed me. Come on, let's go.'

He put her into the sports car and slid in beside her. 'I love you,' he murmured, and then started the engine.

They had dinner at a quiet restaurant in Soho where they could talk. Afterwards they sat for hours over drinks, companionably discussing Caroline's future.

John was quite effusive to begin with and then for a while there was silence between them, each busy with their own thoughts. Then with a muffled groan, John said:

It's no good, Caroline. I've got to ask you now. Will you marry me?'

Caroline, after her conversation with Amanda, was not surprised. She had sensed something like this was about to happen.

'I'll be down from the university next year,' he continued when she did not reply. 'I wanted to wait until then, but after this sudden windfall you've had I was afraid you might go off and meet someone else in the meantime. I know we haven't known each other very long and that you say you don't love me, but I love and need you. This affair has precipitated things and I know we could have a good life together.'

Caroline drew on her cigarette and looked thoughtfully at him. How could she agree to marry him? She would only hurt him in the end.

'You're very sweet, John,' she began slowly. 'I'm really quite fond of you, but there's something you ought to know about your father and me.'

John looked steadily at her. 'I think I already know,' he said softly. 'You were in love with him, weren't you?'

'Yes.'

'I guessed as much, the way you liked me to talk about him. I'd have been blind not to have guessed.'

Caroline flushed. 'I didn't know I was so transparent.'

'You weren't to anyone else,' he replied, sighing, 'but I'm in love with you, Caroline, and I think I know you pretty well.'

'I wonder if you do.' Caroline frowned. 'If you do, you must surely see that I can bring you nothing but unhappiness.'

'Nonsense.' John was angry now. 'If I'm prepared to take the risk, why can't you?'

'You don't understand,' she cried achingly. 'Do you know why we split up?'

'I suppose Dad didn't want to get in too deep,' remarked John quietly. 'I'm sorry if that sounds crude.'

'No, perhaps you're right,' admitted Caroline reflectively. 'He told me I was too young for him, and he was too old for me.'

'Oh.' John looked down at his cigarette. 'Was that the only reason?'

'No. He thought I was going out with another boy while he was in America in November.'

'And were you?'

'Not in the way he thinks. It's a long story. I haven't

the heart to explain it all to you. He wouldn't let me explain it to him.'

'So he was jealous.'

'I suppose so. Oh, John, why am I telling you all this?'

'Because I asked you and because you're getting it out of your system. My father, as you have already learned, is a stubborn man. He is also a fool.'

Caroline flushed. 'I'll take that as a compliment to me,' she said, trying to lighten the conversation.

John sighed. 'And do you still love him?'

'I think so. . .oh, what's the use of lying, I know so.'

'I see.' John looked very thoughtful. 'Doesn't your sudden wealth make any difference?' he asked suddenly.

'Not to my feelings for him, no.' She smiled. 'You see I'm a very poor risk.'

'Not to me,' he replied quietly. 'The way I feel, I'd take you on any terms.'

Caroline shrugged. 'Knowing all this?' she exclaimed in amazement.

'Yes.' John was serious. 'I know you feel very miserable at the moment, but I'm convinced I can change all that. Give me the chance to try.'

Caroline hesitated. She wanted to be fair.

'Give me time to think,' she murmured softly. 'You're going too fast for me.'

'I personally think that you need shaking out of yourself,' he stated firmly. 'I don't believe you feel as deeply for my father as you think you do. He is too old for you. You need a boy of your own age. . . like me.'

Caroline felt immeasurably older than John at that

moment. It was obvious from his words that he had
never felt anything so deeply that nothing could dis-
lodge it. Was it like that with his feelings towards
herself? Might she not hurt herself more than him in
the long run? And that being so, had she the right to
take the risk?

'At least become engaged to me,' he pressed her.
'Let's get that settled.'

Looking at his expectant face, she capitulated. 'All
right,' she agreed softly, and his fingers gripped hers
tightly. 'On one condition,' she continued.

'Which is?' He looked disturbed.

'That either of us may terminate this arrangement
if the need arises.'

'Agreed,' he nodded, relieved that it was nothing
more. 'You won't be sorry. We'll have some wonderful times. And that week in Paris will serve as a
beginning.'

'All right.' Caroline let him carry her along on his
stream of enthusiasm. It was good to have the decisions
made for her. Perhaps now she could relax.

At John's request, Caroline agreed to an engagement
party, but when she found it was to be given at Slayford
on Easter Saturday she wished with all her heart she
had not. John, however, seemed highly pleased with
life and when Caroline expressed her doubts about the
affair he just laughed and said that it was natural that
Adam should give the party for his own son and that
everybody would be suspicious if it was kept a hole-
and-corner affair.

Caroline dreaded the party and the inevitable meeting with Adam. She had hoped that she might have had

longer to get used to the engagement before flaunting it before him like this. Would he think it was her idea?

John had taken the measurement of Caroline's finger and had said that she would be able to choose her ring on the night of the party. They were leaving for Paris on Sunday morning and Caroline was taking all her luggage with her and staying overnight at the villa.

Amanda was very worried about the whole thing, but refused to say anything to her friend. It was obvious that Caroline intended to make her own mistakes and Amanda was convinced that this was the biggest so far.

While they were in Paris, an estate agent who was an associate of Adam Steinbeck and who had been contacted by John was going to find Caroline and Amanda another flat and Caroline had told her friend that she would completely furnish it with new furniture.

Amanda's own excitement at the unexpected gift from Caroline was marred by the events taking place around her, but she did her best to appear cheerful and assisted Caroline in choosing a new wardrobe suitable to her acquired wealth.

Amanda of course was attending the party and she too bought a new dress for the occasion. Caroline's dress was a white pleated chiffon with a high roll collar in front and a deep V-neckline at the back. The bodice was close-fitting with long transparent sleeves which ended in cuffs studded with diamanté, and the skirt was a swirl of pleats.

Caroline sighed as she realised that Adam's good taste had really chosen the dress for her, because she knew he would hate to see her in a cotton caftan such as John favoured. Thus she was dressing for Adam and not her fiancé.

Amanda's dress suited her to perfection; a plain red velvet which somehow did not clash with her vivid hair. Caroline reflected that Amanda seemed much more John's type of girl than she did herself.

John had arranged to collect the girls in his father's Rolls-Royce at seven o'clock and when Caroline awoke on Saturday morning she felt sure she would not survive the ordeal. However, her natural resilience asserted itself and by the evening she had acquired an air of detachment, as though all this was happening to someone else, not Caroline Sinclair.

'I must admit,' remarked Amanda as they waited for the car, 'I'm dying to meet all these rich people. I'm glad you asked me.'

'I need some moral support,' replied Caroline. She knew that Amanda was aware of her earlier trepidation.

'Don't worry,' said Amanda easily, 'you've taken the plunge now, Caroline, and you must think about John. After all, he will be your husband one day. He loves you, and the life you'll lead as his wife won't leave much time for speculation. As for the other. . .' She sighed. 'Things won't always seem as sharply defined as they do today.'

'Spare me the platitudes,' said Caroline, wrapping a cape about her shoulders, uncaring of its silky textutre. 'I think that's the car.'

John was punctual and the two girls went down to meet him. Amanda had not yet been introduced and was very curious. Caroline performed the introductions and watched John's eyebrows ascend at the vivid picture Amanda made. However, after a swift handshake, his eyes were all for Caroline, and Amanda, who had been instantly attracted by his lean good looks, felt rather envious.

John put Caroline in the front of the car and assisted Amanda into the back. Caroline's suitcase was placed in the boot and they were off. Amanda felt quite isolated in the massive rear of the car, but John lowered the glass partition between the seats enabling Amanda to join in their conversation.

The journey to Slayford was soon accomplished, much to Caroline's regret. It was a comparatively warm spring-like evening and the ride had been very pleasant. She moved closer to John as though inviting his support and one of his hands found hers, clasping it in a warm, reassuring grasp. Caroline found herself relaxing. It was wonderful to know John loved her and suddenly the evening lost some of its menace. With John beside her to give her strength she could surely maintain the calm which she had cultivated during the day. After all, what could happen? She would see Adam. So what? He was only a man, after all. And he apparently did not object to their engagement or he would have prevented John from seeing her.

The villa at Slayford sparkled with lights as they turned between the drive gates to find that already the drive was almost filled with parked cars. There were to be twenty guests excluding Adam, Caroline, John and Amanda. Dinner was to be served at eight and it was nearly that already.

The staff had been supplemented for the evening and when they entered the hall a smart young maid took their wraps and directed them to the ladies' powder room.

John went into the lounge to find his father while Caroline and Amanda retouched their make-up and combed their hair. At John's departure, Caroline found her old nervousness returning and delayed her exit from the cloakroom as long as she dared. Amanda was getting impatient, anxious as she was to see round the place and she urged Caroline to hurry. The other women using the room were all beautifully dressed, jewels sparkling in their ears, and around their throats and wrists. Caroline was glad she had chosen to wear the platinum bracelet. At least it compared favourably with the other jewellery on display, she thought wryly.

Back in the hall, John awaited them, accompanied by Adam. The colour receded from Caroline's face when she saw him and she was glad when John gripped her fingers and drew her nearer to him.

Adam looked wonderful in a dinner suit, thought Caroline achingly. He always looked so immaculately turned out, his hair gleaming in the light from the chandelier. He looked so assured and quite undisturbed by her arrival. The knife turned in the wound!

'Hello, Caroline,' he said gravely, a rather cynical glint in his dark eyes. 'I understand congratulations are in order. I hope you'll both be very happy.'

'Thank you.' Caroline almost choked over the word, feeling nausea sweep over her. It was all assuming the proportions of a nightmare that couldn't possibly be happening and she had a sudden urge to scream that she wasn't going to marry anybody and run from this place as swiftly as her legs would carry her. But she quelled the hysteria, recognising it for what it was, and as common sense prevailed she managed to stand apparently calm as John introduced Amanda to his father.

She saw Amanda's eyes widen as she shook hands with the big man and thought bitterly that Adam attracted women as naturally as the flame attracts the moth.

During the course of the evening, Caroline was introduced to a great number of people, some relatives and some just close friends. She knew she would never remember all their names, but they all seemed friendly enough and willing to accept her into their charmed circle.

Dinner was served in the big dining-room and afterwards John took Caroline into the library to choose her ring.

The table in the centre of the room was covered with trays of rings in all colours, stones and settings. Caroline was completely astounded and gasped.

'John!' she exclaimed. 'They must be worth a fortune. Why on earth did you get so many?'

'I wanted you to have plenty to choose from,' he replied smiling. 'I don't get engaged every day, and besides, you can have them all if you'd like them.'

Caroline shook her head. 'Oh, John,' she whispered, 'you're much too good to me.'

'I only want the best for you,' he replied softly. 'Come on. Try some on.'

Each ring was exquisite in its own particular way. The stones were perfect, the settings merely enhancing the beauty of the main jewel. Caroline was completely overawed. It was at times like this that she realised just how different were their backgrounds.

At last she said: 'You choose, John. Please. I can't.'

John considered the rings thoughtfully. 'If you really want it that way, I choose this one.' The ring was an emerald, set among diamonds in a circle of platinum. 'It's the green of your eyes,' he told her softly, and slid it on to her finger. As with all the rings, the fit was perfect, and he nodded approvingly. 'Do you like it?' he murmured, kissing her cheek.

'Yes,' she breathed, and knowing he wanted it, she turned her mouth to his.

A few minutes later he put her away from him. 'Good,' he said, smiling. 'Now, let's go and show everybody.'

In their absence, the lounge had been cleared for dancing. The carpet had been rolled back from the polished floor and a record player was already giving out modern music. One or two couples were already dancing. Caroline could see Amanda dancing with an elderly man with a handlebar moustache whom John had introduced as Sir Ralph Marchman, a local politician.

When John and Caroline appeared they were soon surrounded by well-wishers wanting to see the ring, and congratulations came thick and fast. John was slapped enthusiastically on the back and the usual jokes were made about Caroline having trapped John at last. Champagne was brought in in huge buckets of ice and everyone drank their health, including Adam, whose eyes were broodingly intense when they met Caroline's over the heads of the others and she felt herself tremble.

When the music began again, Adam pushed his way through the people surrounding them and said:

'I think I'm entitled to the first dance, Caroline.'

No one but John was aware of any significance in his words and he had no choice, in the face of all these people, but to let her go with good grace.

So Caroline found herself again in Adam's arms, conscious of a strange feeling of having come home. This was where she belonged. Why did Adam choose to be so blind?

They danced in silence for a while, giving Caroline time to compose herself. It was difficult trying to be calm when your whole body trembled at the touch of the man you were dancing with and ached for a closer contact still. After a while she gave up trying to rationalise things and simply enjoyed the sensation.

Then he said: 'I hear you are now a rich young woman.'

'Comparatively so,' she agreed softly. 'I feel quite light-headed about the whole thing.'

'Is that why you've got yourself engaged to John?' he demanded savagely.

'I'd rather not discuss that with you,' she replied shakily.

'I'll bet you wouldn't,' he retorted angrily. 'Caroline, why are you doing this to me?'

'Adam,' she breathed, forcing herself to stay calm with an effort, 'we have nothing to say to one another.'

'No?' he asked coldly. 'Wouldn't you like to know my feelings in all this? Don't you want to know whether I still love you?'

'Don't,' she whispered achingly. 'It's over, Adam.'

Adam shrugged his broad shoulders and drew her closer against him.

'Is it?' he muttered harshly, feeling her trembling body.

Ignoring his question she said: 'I hear you're flying to America in a few days.'

'Yes.' He frowned. 'My mother will be interested to hear all about John's engagement. She would have liked to come over, but she's had an attack of rheumatism and couldn't face the journey.' He looked down at her. 'And you and John are going to Paris?'

'Yes. By the way, I'm no longer an employee of the Steinbeck Corporation. I've sent in my resignation. I got a very nice letter back this morning from Mr Lawson. He seemed sorry to lose me.'

'And what do you intend to do after John returns to Radbury?'

'I don't know yet. I haven't made any definite plans.'

'I see.'

They danced in silence again, until Caroline stumbled, not thinking of what she was doing.

'I'm sorry,' she said, meaning her default, but Adam's face darkened ominously.

'Are you? For everything?'

'I don't understand you,' she said imploringly. 'You didn't want me when you had the chance. Why are you tormenting me now?'

'I did want you,' he replied coldly. 'I simply didn't want to spoil your life. Instead you're spoiling it for yourself.'

'Why do you say that? John and I will have a good life.'

'For a time, maybe,' he conceded slowly. 'But you're under an illusion about John, I'm afraid. He's not the constant type. I should know.'

'Adam!' Her voice was suddenly angry. 'How dare you say that?'

'It's true,' he replied quietly. 'Oh, I know he's been taking you to symphony concerts and the opera and completely playing the classical gentleman, but it won't last. At least, I don't think it will, and I don't want you to get hurt.'

Caroline laughed hysterically for a moment and then sobered.

'Imagine you saying a thing like that,' she exclaimed, 'the master of the art of hurting me!'

With a blare of trumpets the music ended and Caroline drew forcefully away from Adam. Swaying slightly, she made her way back to John's side, only aware of needing his support and nearness as her legs turned to jelly beneath her. She thought for a moment she was going to faint, but the feeling passed and she grasped John's arm tightly and said:

'Don't make me dance with your father any more, please, John.'

John put his arm around her, concerned at her pallor. 'All right,' he said, wondering just what Adam had been saying to cause such a furore in the girl at his side.

Later in the evening, Caroline saw Amanda dancing with Adam. She was obviously having a wonderful time and was thoroughly enjoying herself. She was laughing at something Adam had said and Caroline found she couldn't bear to watch them. She was very relieved when at last the party broke up and she could escape to her room.

CHAPTER SEVEN

ADAM offered to drive Amanda home in the Rolls as most of the guests lived nearby or further out of London and Amanda had expected to have to call a taxi. She was therefore flattered and pleased that he should offer.

As they drove along the darkened country roads she said:

'I have enjoyed myself, Mr Steinbeck.'

Adam smiled, lighting a cigar. 'I'm glad,' he said, and then with a frown he asked, 'Tell me, is Caroline really happy?'

Amanda clasped her hands tightly round her evening bag. With a wry grimace she realised that Adam had asked to take her home simply to talk about Caroline. It was galling, but she accepted it without rancour. She too was worried about her friend. It was quite a relief to discuss it with somebody.

'I would hardly call her happy,' she said carefully. 'But I think perhaps this is the best way, after all. This new interest in her life might make all the difference.'

'But what about the money?' exclaimed Adam. 'Wasn't she thrilled with the unlimited prospects she could think about?'

'I don't think she cares about money, one way or the other,' replied Amanda truthfully. 'Caroline is a very emotional person. Her feelings seem to be more important somehow. She's been badly hurt and I for one want her normal again.'

Adam's teeth clenched on the cigar. Everything he had heard tonight seemed to point to the fact that Caroline was trying to escape from unhappiness by plunging herself into a web of deceit. Was John aware of the true facts of their relationship? Could it be possible that he, Adam, had been mistaken about her? There were a thousand questions he wanted to ask this girl, but this was not the time or the place. Besides, how could he be sure that the answers she gave were the right answers? He was only able to get those sort of answers from Caroline and she was too much on the defensive with him ever to be willing to bare her heart to him again.

One last question he was forced to ask. 'Would you say that she was mature for her years?' he asked softly.

Amanda shrugged. 'I don't think I can answer that,' she replied. 'Why don't you ask her these questions, Mr Steinbeck?'

'Would I get the right answers, do you think?' he asked wryly.

'Then leave her alone altogether,' said Amanda, forgetting herself and her manners for a moment. 'Give her a chance to find out for herself what is important and what isn't.'

Adam was not offended. 'Yes,' he said thoughtfully, 'perhaps you're right.'

As he drove back to Slayford his mind was plagued with thoughts, each one chasing the other round his head. There was still the painful business of Mark Davison which had never been explained away. True, he had not allowed her to explain when she had wanted

to, but what could she have said? To his tired mind
there was no possible explanation, except that she had
been bored, and that only proved his original opinion.
She was too young.

But as the car neared Slayford and he remembered
the feel of her in his arms that evening, he felt his
whole body yearn for her and her nearness and he was
inexplicably glad that they were leaving for Paris in
the morning.

Meanwhile, as Amanda undressed and got into bed
she pondered on his words. From his manner and conversation she believed he was in love with Caroline
even if he did not intend to do anything about it. How
could he let his own son marry her when he felt the
way he did? He was either very unselfish or completely
uncaring, and she didn't believe the latter for a
moment. But couldn't he see that Caroline was the
truthful kind and that the business over Mark Davison
must have a logical explanation? Remembering her
friend in the early days of her relationship with Adam
Steinbeck, Amanda sighed. Caroline had been so gay
and happy. So sure of herself, and now she was uncertain and unhappy.

Now that she had met Adam Steinbeck she could
understand Caroline's feelings for him. He was very
attractive physically, of course, but more than that, he
gave you a feeling of being protected and cared for in
his presence. His very obvious personality was warm
and friendly and he seemed to be interested in everything you said. You forgot he was the Chairman of
the Steinbeck Corporation and acted quite naturally
with him. To be loved by him must be a wonderful

thing, thought Amanda, sighing, before she drew the covers up to her chin.

As for John Steinbeck, Amanda was not sure. He was pleasant enough, she supposed, and certainly more her line of country. He didn't expect too intelligent a conversation and it had been obvious from his treatment of her that he liked an attractive woman, even if he was engaged.

She could understand him. He was open and young and rather a devil. She was sure he had found her attractive and the thought worried her, on Caroline's behalf.

Caroline heard the Rolls-Royce come up the drive, the swish of the wheels on the gravel. She had known he was taking Amanda home and couldn't prevent the feeling of envy she felt at the knowledge. What would they talk about? Did Adam find Amanda attractive? She was sure Amanda found him so. She lay awake until about four o'clock. She wished she could sleep. She had a big day ahead of her tomorrow. The trip to Paris looming on the horizon. When at last she did fall asleep it seemed no time before Mrs Jones was drawing back the curtains and saying 'Good morning' in her bright and breezy manner.

She placed a tray across Caroline's knees as she struggled up into a sitting position and said:

'John thought you might prefer this to rushing down to the dining-room.'

'Thank you so much,' said Caroline, managing a smile. 'I do prefer it today. I still feel rather tired.'

'You look very peaky, I must say,' remarked Mrs

Jones candidly. 'I hope you're not sickening for 'flu or something.'

'So do I,' said Caroline, sighing. 'Anyway, I expect it was last night's party. Maybe I overdid it.'

'No such thing at your age,' exclaimed Mrs Jones. 'No, I think you must be a little run down, miss. You take things easy on this holiday. Don't go rushing round that there French place and knocking yourself up.'

Caroline chuckled. 'All right, Mrs Jones. It's nice of you to concern yourself with me.'

'Not at all. You're almost one of the family now, although things haven't turned out as I expected.' There was an awkward pause and then she hurried on: 'But you enjoy your breakfast, love, and don't worry about a thing.'

After she had gone, Caroline poured herself a cup of coffee. As she stirred it she thought again what a nice person Mrs Jones was. No wonder Adam and John thought a lot of her. She was more like a member of the family herself. Caroline wondered just what she did think about the situation here. After all, she had met Caroline originally through Adam and perhaps she had hoped the master was going to re-marry at last.

Adam was not around when Caroline and John left in the chauffeur-driven Rolls. John had seen him earlier before he left to go riding, but Caroline had not spoken to him since the previous evening during that disastrous dance. This morning Caroline was wearing a slim-fitting suit of cherry-red wool and a loose cream mohair coat. John complimented her upon her appearance and she felt glad when they were settled in the back of the car and actually on their way.

As the car passed the end of the Steinbeck estate, a horseman in a dark blue sweater and jodhpurs could be seen in the distance watching them and Caroline shivered as she recognised Adam's broad frame. Even at this distance he looked magnificent, a black stallion rearing beneath him.

John looked reflectively at her as they took the main London road, and then, leaning forward, he kissed her cheek.

'I love you,' he murmured softly.

Caroline managed a small smile. 'Do you, John? Oh, I'm glad we're leaving England for a while. It will make all the difference!'

'Of course it will,' said John confidently, and Caroline wondered whether he felt as assured as he tried to make out.

The hotel in Paris lived up to all Caroline's expectations. John had booked a suite of rooms, but as there were two bedrooms, each with its own bathroom, Caroline did not attach any significance to this. She was too bemused by the richness of her surroundings to ponder John's newly acquired posessiveness. She was eager to explore outside the hotel, too, the treasures of the city beckoning her insistently.

But in this she found John less than co-operative. He had seen it all before, and it was not in his scheme of things that they should spend their time wandering round historical monuments. It soon became clear that his reason for bringing her to Paris were much more personal ones.

At the beginning of the week, Caroline was prepared to humour him, allowing him to take the initiative, but quelling quite drastically any ideas he might have had to make their relationship a more intimate one. Whether John thought time would change her mind, she wasn't sure, but certainly it was not too difficult to keep their relationship on a friendly basis. It was only when some particular thing infuriated him that Caroline glimpsed a different side to her companion, one of sulky, bored petulance, that disturbed her quite a lot.

As a car was at their disposal, they visited Fontainebleau, the Renaissance palace set in exquisitely designed gardens. Caroline was enchanted, but John spent the afternoon making sardonic comments, and thoroughly destroyed Caroline's interest.

The following day they drove out of Paris again, this time on some expedition of John's. As Caroline had begged for their visit to Fontainebleau, John had insisted that he decide their plans for the following day.

They parked the car in woodlands, beside a swiftly flowing stream, where beds of wild flowers provided carpets of yellow and blue and violet. They left the car, walking down to the water's edge, where Caroline dabbled her hands in the stream.

'It's a beautiful spot,' she said, as John pulled a rug out of the car and threw it on the grass for them to sit on.

'Yes, isn't it?' John sounded pleased with himself. He flung himself on the rug, stretching lazily. 'Come here, Caroline.'

Caroline sighed. 'Why, John? I'm not tired. Couldn't we walk through the woods some way?'

John rolled on to his side. 'Are you afraid of me, Caroline?'

She stood up. 'Of course not.' This wasn't the first

time John had attempted to interrogate her in this way. She imagined he was endeavouring to arouse either her indignation or her enthusiasm, but he was not succeeding.

'Caroline,' he said again, 'this situation of ours has got to develop, you realise that, don't you?'

'Develop, John?' Caroline was being deliberately obtuse.

'Don't play with me, Caroline!' He sounded a little less amiable now.

'Oh, John, I'm not playing!' Caroline lifted her shoulders. 'You're going too fast. This trip to France was supposed to be a holiday. As it is, it's turning into a contest and you think you're going to win!'

John sprang up and came over to her. 'This is serious, Caroline. I'm only human, and you're a tease!' He pressed his lips to hers passionately.

'I don't know what you mean,' she replied, trying to release herself.

'Oh, yes, you do,' he muttered. 'Caroline, I've told you, I'm in love with you. What more can I say?'

Caroline bit her lip. 'John. . .' she began, but he had released her and returned to his position on the rug.

'Come and sit down,' he said pleadingly. 'Caroline, what are you afraid of? We're engaged. I'm not some stranger who's brought you out here to seduce you.'

Caroline hesitated for a moment and then she went over and sat down beside him on the rug. She felt strangely upset. After all, they were engaged, and John had always been kind and thoughtful towards her.

'That's better,' said John, smiling and drawing her back beside him. 'Now,' he said, his mouth inches above hers, 'kiss me, Caro.'

Caroline was about to say something when his mouth descended on hers and pressed hard. She was too nervously disturbed to respond, but John didn't seem to notice and she felt his hands caressing her urgently.

'Don't,' she whispered, when he released her mouth, but John did not heed her. With a stifled moan she twisted away, so quickly that John released her at once and she jumped on to her feet and ran to the car. Breathing swiftly, she pulled open the door and got into her seat and sat there smoothing her hair, uncaring of what he was doing.

It seemed like hours before he joined her, when actually it was only a few moments. He slung the rug into the back and slid behind the wheel. Caroline hardly dared to look at him. What now? He leant heavily on the steering wheel and then looked her way.

'Well,' he said with a sigh, 'I guess I should apologise.'

Caroline shrugged helplessly. 'What can I say?' she said, running a hand through her hair. 'I suppose I'm to blame really. But don't expect too much, too soon.'

'All right.' He nodded. 'I realise I'm rushing you. I'm sorry. I suppose I never had much patience where girls were concerned.'

'You mean you've never had to wait before, is that it?'

Caroline's voice was light, but there was an undertone of seriousness.

'I guess you might say that.' John started the car's engine, and there the conversation ended for the time being.

For the remainder of their stay John was as circum-

spect as she could have wished, but the relationship
between them was most definitely strained. It was as
though that incident in the middle of the week had
altered everything between them. They no longer had
anything to say to one another, and Caroline was sure
John was beginning to see the futility of their engagement. It was all her fault really. She ought never to
have allowed him to talk her into it. It had been a
crazy idea right from the start, and because mentally,
if not actually physically, she was older than he was,
she ought to have had more sense. Her own selfishness
at clinging to John because of his father was troubling
her, particularly as it seemed John was no different
from any other young man, and his protestations of
love had been based on an egotistical belief that she
would not be able to go on thinking of Adam while
John was making love to her. But it wasn't true, and
now he knew it, too.

They returned to London and on their first evening
they had a meal at the flat with Amanda. She was full
of news of a new flat that the estate agent had found
for them and was eager for Caroline to see it. It was
situated in a new block not far from Gloucester Court,
with two bedrooms, a lounge and kitchen, and its own
bathroom. After the months of sharing that would be
heaven, thought Caroline.

Amanda had made a chicken curry for supper to
celebrate and they ate companionably, talking about
Paris and the places they had visited. Amanda was
very interested, but she was well aware of the tension
between them. Both addressed Amanda more than each
other and she felt uncomfortably as though she was
playing gooseberry. However, there was nothing she

could do except go to bed when supper was over, pleading a headache.

John helped Caroline with the dishes and then they went back into the lounge for a final cigarette.

'Well,' he said, 'where shall we go tomorrow?'

Caroline shrugged. 'Is your father staying away long?'

'At least a fortnight, I imagine,' replied John, with a sigh. 'Why?'

'No reason. I wondered whether you intended going to see your grandmother.'

'Oh,' John shrugged. 'I don't suppose I'll go this vac. I only have another ten days before I go back to the pen.'

Caroline smiled, 'I'm sure you enjoy it really.'

'Are you? Oh, well, I suppose I do enjoy the laughs and the comradeship.'

'There you are, then.' She drew on her cigarette. 'Where would you like to go tomorrow?'

After John had gone, Amanda came out of the bedroom in her dressing gown.

'Well,' she said forthrightly. 'What's wrong now?'

Caroline shrugged. 'If I tell you you'll only say I told you so.'

'I see.' Amanda frowned. 'What's happened to make you change your mind?'

'Numerous things,' said Caroline vaguely, and then: 'Oh, Mandy, he tried to make love to me and I wouldn't let him.'

Amanda sighed. 'It was only to be expected. He's that sort.'

'Don't say that,' cried Caroline. 'He's supposed to

be in love with me. As it is I feel as though that's all he's interested in.'

'Now that is silly,' reproved Amanda. 'I wonder what you would have thought if you'd been in love with him.'

'That's the awful part,' agreed Caroline, sighing. 'I think I would have been different. As it was I felt frigid and I know he thought I was an idiot.'

'Well, that can't be helped. Honey, don't do anything which can't be remedied. When you give yourself to a man be sure it's because you want to and not because you only want to please him.'

Caroline felt utterly dejected. The trip which had held such promise had turned out to be a flop and now she didn't even want to see John very much. In the days that followed, she gave her whole mind to the new flat. It was exactly as Amanda had described and Caroline spent hours designing the fittings. It gave her something to do and she had plenty of money to spend on it. She knew the nominal rent had been fixed by Adam and the thought cheered her a little. At least he had been kind enough to see to that before he went away.

She met John every day and spent many hours with him. He remained unusually reserved, but Caroline was too reserved herself to care very much. When Amanda was available she invited her to join them and Amanda found John turning more to her than Caroline for conversation. She didn't know what to do. She felt the usurper and yet they wanted it that way.

When John returned to Radbury, Caroline felt unconscionably relieved. At least she could now have the opportunity to collect her thoughts without needing to interrupt them by meeting John. How could she look at things objectively with him by her side? It was better for both of them that a separation should take place.

The two girls moved into the newly-furnished flat within two days of John's departure. Amanda was very impressed by the wall-to-wall carpeting and modern kitchen equipment. A huge television graced one alcove while a stereo-radiogram graced the other. Everything was there for luxuriously comfortable living and Amanda was thrilled. She had offered to share the expense, but Caroline wanted to do it all herself, and besides, as she said, she could well afford it. The house at Hampstead Heath had been sold for a terrific figure to a syndicate of companies interested in land development, and it wasn't until after the deal had gone through that Caroline found it had been bought by the Steinbeck Corporation.

She wrote to John as usual, but his letters were fewer than in the early days of their relationship. She felt sure he was regretting the affair as much as she was and wished something had been said before he returned to college. However, something was to happen which was to make her glad she was still considered engaged to John.

After spending a few days drifting round the flat feeling aimless, she suddenly decided to take a trip to Greece. She had long wanted to visit that country and now that she was fancy-free there was nothing to stop her.

She made all the arrangements with Amanda's approval and booked her flight in advance. The evening before she was due to leave she wrote to John explaining about the trip and also offering him his freedom if that was what he wanted. It was a difficult letter to write and each attempt looked worse than the last. She had just begun her fourth attempt when the telephone pealed beside her.

She was still unused to this new innovation in her home and she jumped at the unaccustomed sound. Sliding off her chair, she crossed the room and picked up the receiver, giving the number automatically.

'Is that you, Miss Sinclair?' For a moment she did not recognise the voice, then she said: 'Is that you, Mrs Jones?'

'Yes, miss. Oh, I'm so glad you're in. I've been trying to contact John without any success and then I remembered that Mr Steinbeck had this number in his book. He arranged it all with Mr Mason, didn't he?'

Mr Mason was the estate agent.

'Yes, that's right, Mrs Jones. What is it? What's wrong?'

'I've had a telephone call from Mrs Steinbeck, miss, from Boston. She too had tried to contact John, but without doing so, so she called me. Calls from America are so expensive and she couldn't keep on ringing from that distance.'

'But what's it all about?' asked Caroline, a cold hand seeming to close round her heart.

'It's Mr Steinbeck, miss. He's had a motor car accident and apparently he's in hospital, near his mother's home. They live just outside Boston, a place called Roseberry, and there's a big hospital there.'

Caroline's legs gave way beneath her and she sank down on to a chair by the telephone.

'Is. . .is he badly hurt, Mrs Jones?'

'Mrs Steinbeck said he'd been cut about the face

and he'd gashed his left arm pretty badly. They were still unsure about internal injuries.'

'Oh, Mrs Jones!' Caroline felt violently sick. This, to happen to her beloved Adam. It was too much.

'There, miss, don't you go upsetting yourself. These things always sound worse than they really are.'

Caroline shivered. 'Mrs Jones, do you have any idea what a shock this has been?'

'I think so,' replied the older woman. 'I always thought you were more fitting to Mr Adam than to young John. He's too flibberty-gibbety. I think the world of him, of course, but I'm not blind to his faults!'

'Then will you give me Mrs Steinbeck's address?' asked Caroline, making a sudden decision.

Mrs Jones did not hesitate. 'What do you intend to do?' she asked when Caroline had written the address down.

'I'll leave a message for John, and let him know, and then I'm going to try and make arrangements to go to Boston.'

Mrs Jones sighed. 'I'm so glad, miss, really I am. And I'm sure Mr Adam will be pleased to see you.'

'Do you think so? Do you really think so?' exclaimed Caroline.

'Of course, miss. I've noticed the change in him these last few months. We know him too well to be mistaken.'

Suddenly Caroline realised that she was discussing Adam with his housekeeper, and that would never do. After warm goodbyes she rang off, and sat staring at the telephone for a moment.

Then she marshalled her thoughts. There was nothing she could do until the morning. She would need a visa to enter the United States, and she could only get that from the American Embassy. Still, there was no harm in making enquiries about flights from London Airport.

After ringing the airport, she rang John's rooms at Radbury and although she couldn't speak to John because he was out she left a message with his landlady. She wondered where he could be. He was supposed to be inundated with work for his exams, but obviously he had taken the evening off. Maybe he was out with a girl. The thought did not disturb her as it should.

When Amanda returned home, Caroline was pacing the floor restlessly, smoking cigarette after cigarette. Amanda frowned when she saw the littered ashtrays.

'What's wrong?' she asked. 'Having cold feet about tomorrow?'

The trip to Greece had gone out of Caroline's head, and she stared at her friend uncomprehendingly for a moment.

'Heavens! I'd forgotten! I'll have to cancel the arrangements!'

'Cancel them?' echoed Amanda blankly. 'Why?'

Caroline explained, and Amanda shook her head. 'And you think this is the right thing to do? I mean, don't you think you ought to wait and ask for John's advice?'

'John and I are finished,' said Caroline heavily. 'I— I've been trying to write to him tonight. As it is—it will have to wait.'

Amanda felt impatient, and then she sighed. 'All right. It seems there's no point in my saying anything. You've made up your mind, haven't you?'

'Yes.' Caroline stubbed out her cigarette decisively. 'I'm only grateful to Aunt Barbara for providing me with this money. For the first time in my life it's going to do me a little good!'

Teresa Steinbeck entered the wide, sunlit room which her son was occupying in the Roseberry Hospital and smiled at Adam cheerfully. She was a tall, well-dressed woman in her early sixties, and looked considerably younger. Only rheumatism threatened her otherwise youthful appearance, and Adam looked at her with affection. Dressed in a heavy silk suit of palest pink, she looked slim and attractive, and most concerned.

'Well, darling,' she said, closing the door and walking to the side of his bed, 'how are you feeling now?'

'Much better,' said Adam with an attempt at a smile. It was painful to move his face at the moment owing to the stitches he had had in his left cheek. His face was partially bandaged and his arm was bound up too. However, apart from a slight pallor he looked quite well.

'Good.' Teresa nodded thankfully. When she had first had the news of the accident she had been terribly upset, but now that the specialist had found no internal injuries she felt much easier in her mind. It had been such an awful thing to happen. Three teenagers in a big convertible losing control of their car and careering across the freeway into Adam's saloon. It was lucky he hadn not been killed, but fortunately no one was seriously hurt. His face might be scarred, of course, but plastic surgery could work wonders.

'Did you hear from John?' asked Adam, frowning.

'I wish you hadn't rung him really, you know. It wasn't necessary.'

'Nonsense. A boy should know when his own father is in hospital.'

'It depends on the father,' replied Adam dryly. 'John and I haven't had too much to say to one another lately.'

Teresa shook her head irritably. 'Stop concerning yourself over the boy. Let him have a bit of worry for a change. Do him good. Becoming too selfish, so he is. Couldn't even bring this girl to meet me before he got himself engaged to her.'

Adam's eyes darkened. 'Mother, that's John's affair. Don't interfere.'

Teresa's eyes twinkled. 'But that's what I am, didn't you know?' she chuckled, 'an interfering old woman.'

Adam looked indulgently at his mother. She didn't know the full facts about John's engagement and perhaps it was just as well. She wouldn't have approved.

'I don't believe that any more than you do,' he replied easily. 'However, let's skip it. When are they letting me out of this place?'

'I spoke to Doctor Morgan before I came to see you, and he said that after the stitches were removed you might be allowed home. I think they're afraid you might suffer from after-effects of the shock.'

Adam frowned irritably. It wasn't in his nature to enjoy lying in a bed all day and he longed to get up and leave.

'That's almost a week in here,' he muttered with a sigh. 'My God, when they get you into these places they don't care much for getting you out. They must make a fortune that way.'

'Now, Adam,' said his mother placatingly, 'you were glad enough of their help a couple of days ago.'

'Maybe so, but I've had enough now.'

Mrs Steinbeck smiled serenely. 'Well, you're staying here until they discharge you, like it or not. Good heavens, you've no emergency waiting for you. They didn't expect you back in England for at least another week.'

'All right.' Adam gave up trying to argue with her. It was no use anyway. Until the stitches were removed it was easier to stay where he was.

The house owned by Teresa Steinbeck stood in Roseberry Drive. It was a massive, palatial mansion which had originally been owned by an American oil tycoon. When Adam purchased the house for her she had been overawed by the size of it, but now she was used to it she really loved the building. The end of the road joined a highway which ran beside the cliffs over-looking Roseberry Sound. A wide beach stretched down to the water which shelved away swiftly and was dangerous for swimming, but the musical sound of the sea could always be heard in the houses in Roseberry Drive, and Teresa, who came from Western Ireland, was nostalgically reminded of her beloved Galway.

When Teresa arrived home, driving herself in the big saloon, her coloured maid, Liza, met her in the marble hallway.

'There's a young lady awaiting to see you, ma'am,' she said worriedly. 'She says her name is Miss Caroline Sinclair and she's English.'

Teresa frowned. She pulled off her gloves and

placed them on the hall table. As she did so the name struck a chord in her memory.

'Sinclair, Sinclair,' she murmured thoughtfully. 'I believe that's the name Adam called John's fiancée, Caroline Sinclair. Is John here, too?'

'No, ma'am. Just this young lady.'

'I see. Well, where is she?'

'I put her in the lounge, ma'am. I offered her tea, but she wouldn't have any.'

'Very well, Liza. Bring us some tea in about ten minutes, will you?'

'Yes, ma'am.'

Teresa frowned and crossed the hall to the lounge. This was certainly an unexpected occurrence, unless of course John was ill also and had sent this girl in his place. Opening one of the double white doors she entered the lounge and closed the door behind her. A tall, slim girl was standing by the open French windows, surveying the gardens, now brilliant with colour. She turned as Teresa came in and Teresa thought she had never seen such a beautiful creature. Her long, almost straight fair hair framed a piquantly attractive face in which green eyes dominated her other features. She looked poignantly sad and Teresa felt it was her grief which added to her allure.

'Miss Sinclair,' she said, advancing into the room, holding out a hand.

'Yes.' Caroline shook hands with her. 'You must be Adam's mother. He's very like you.'

Mrs Steinbeck indicated that she should take a seat and Caroline did so.

'Well, what can I do for you?' asked Teresa, seating herself opposite, and offering Caroline a cigarette.

'Are you John's fiancée, by any chance?'

'At the moment,' said Caroline quietly. 'But before you ask me any questions, how is Adam?'

'My son is in Roseberry Hospital,' replied Teresa, completely intrigued by all this. 'He had facial injuries and a severely lacerated arm, but otherwise he is all right. There were no internal injuries as was suspected at first.'

'Thank God!' murmured Caroline, feeling relief sweep over her.

Teresa was completely baffled. If this girl was engaged to John, she was abnormally concerned about his father, whom she couldn't know so well, surely! It was most unusual.

'I expect you're wondering where John is?' said Caroline, drawing on her cigarette.

Teresa shrugged. 'Miss Sinclair, or may I call you Caroline?' Caroline nodded and she continued: 'you have me at a distinct disadvantage. I don't understand at all what this is about. I can understand that John would be very concerned about his father, but as he is obviously not with you at the moment I can't comprehend why you have come alone. Is John ill?'

'No. He's not ill. In fact, I expect when he received your message he too decided to come out here. But Mrs Jones couldn't contact him yesterday evening when you rang, and so she called me. I'm afraid I dropped everything and flew out here immediately. I wanted to see Adam.'

Teresa sighed, still unable to get the full picture.

'Well,' she said slowly, 'I'm sure that can be arranged. But if you've flown all the way from London, surely you must be tired and hungry.'

Caroline half-smiled. 'Tired, yes; but hungry, no,' she replied. 'Thank you all the same.'

Teresa shrugged helplessly. She sensed instinctively that this girl felt something more than friendship for her son and although she was engaged to her grandson she believed that Caroline was not playing any underhand game. She was too genuinely concerned about Adam. Teresa's innate generosity asserted itself and she said:

'As you're here, you're very welcome to stay for a few days if you would like to. At least until Adam gets out of hospital. And of course, if John arrives he will stay too.'

'Mrs Steinbeck, I feel I should explain,' began Caroline awkwardly, aware of how strange this must all seem to Adam's mother.

'Later,' said Teresa, suddenly standing up. 'Look, you have your reasons for coming here and although I'm sure they concern my son very strongly, I'd rather you rested before attempting to tell me anything. I've just come from the hospital, so we can both go later and see Adam.'

Caroline found tears welling in her eyes. The tension of the last few hours had been almost more than she could bear and now this kindness Adam's mother was showing her proved too much and to her embarrassment she burst into tears.

Teresa moved away, allowing her a few moments of privacy. It was good to cry and clear all tensions from your system. Within a couple of minutes Caroline was composed again and she said:

'Please forgive me. I'm not normally so dramatic. It's simply that I've been so worried.'

'Don't apologise, my dear,' replied Teresa with a smile. 'I, too, gave in to tears when I found he wasn't badly hurt. Women are funny that way.' She turned. 'Ah. . .some tea. Thank you, Liza.'

Liza wheeled in the trolley and smiled at Caroline. Caroline thought she looked a jolly sort of person and she imagined she must be very happy working for as nice a person as Mrs Steinbeck.

After Liza had gone, Teresa poured out the tea and handed a cup to Caroline. After pouring another for herself she said:

'Tell me one thing, Caroline. How long have you known Adam?'

Caroline flushed. 'About six months,' she answered quietly.

'And you and John have only been going out together since January, according to Adam.'

'Yes.'

Caroline was well aware of what this questioning proved.

'So you knew Adam before you knew John,' concluded Teresa.

'Yes.'

'I see. That explains a lot.' Teresa frowned, and bit her lip suddenly. She was recalling a visit Adam had made to America in November of last year. At that time he had accidentally mentioned a girl he had taken to see the house at Slayford. He had not enlarged upon the fact, though, and his mother had been given the impression that he had not intended to mention her at all. She sipped her tea reflectively. Could this possibly be the same girl? Teresa's mind buzzed with the idea. Was that the connection? Had she met John through

Adam and preferred the younger man? That was possible. But then Adam had been on his yacht in the Caribbean in January, so that couldn't be right. She was stumped.

She thought how like Adam it was not to confide in her if that was the case. He had never been one to broadcast his feelings for any woman and his marriage seemed to have made him immune to any serious affection for any female. She had given up hope of him ever remarrying and with John taking no interest in the company it seemed it would pass out of Steinbeck hands during the next generation.

Caroline, watching the play of emotions on Mrs Steinbeck's face, realised what must be going through her mind. She was a shrewd woman and somehow Caroline felt she would not be put off with anything less than the truth.

Finishing her tea, Caroline replaced her cup on the trolley and waited for Adam's mother to make the next move. She felt desperately tired now and felt she could sleep if she was given the opportunity.

Mrs Steinbeck smiled and getting up she walked to the door and opened it. She called: 'Liza!' and a few moments later the coloured maid reappeared. 'Show Miss Sinclair to the guest room,' she said. 'Where is her luggage?'

'Miss Sinclair's suitcase is waiting in the hall, ma'am,' replied Liza. 'I'll take it up. Will you follow me, Miss Sinclair.'

Caroline nodded and rose to her feet. As she reached Mrs Steinbeck she looked thankfully at her.

'I can't thank you enough,' she said, selfconsciously.

Teresa shrugged her slim shoulders. 'You're most welcome, my dear. Besides, I like you and I'm sure we're going to be friends.' She glanced at her watch. 'It's only four-thirty. You can rest for a couple of hours, then we'll have an early meal before going to the hospital.'

Caroline put her hand in the older woman's for a moment, expressing without words her gratitude, and then followed Liza up the wide, fan-shaped staircase. She was shown to a cool, blue room whose wide windows opened on to a balcony which overlooked the gardens at the rear of the building. From the balcony you could catch a glimpse of the azure blue sea in the Sound and the tide could be heard as it came in, thundering on the shore. It sounded soothing and restful, and after Liza had gone, Caroline flung herself on the bed, only stopping to remove her jacket. She was completely exhausted. The last few hours had taken their toll of her and it was good to relax for a while. She fell asleep almost immediately and was awakened by Liza at half-past six.

She felt wonderfully refreshed and took a shower in the adjoining bathroom before dressing in a green, pleated Tricel dress. She applied only a little lipstick, but her fingers trembled continually at the thought of seeing Adam in such a short time. She found her way down to the lounge, but as it was deserted she stepped on to the terrace and looked at the spectacular view. Roseberry Drive was quite high above the small town which lay in a valley and an uninterrupted view of lush greenery and bright flowers quite took your breath away. The air was sweet with the smell of stocks and Caroline took a deep breath, shaking away the cobwebs which her nap had left with her.

Somewhere, not too far away, Adam was probably dining also and within an hour or so she would see him, speak to him, even touch him. The thought was breathtaking. She wondered what he would say, what she would say to him. It was frightening; somehow she had got to convince him she was sincere. She loved him; she would always love him. She couldn't go on living without him. She might as well be dead. Life would no longer have a meaning. It was terrifying to love someone so much.

CHAPTER EIGHT

WHEN Teresa came into the lounge, she saw Caroline standing on the terrace and called her in.

'Will you join me in a glass of sherry?' she asked, pouring some into a crystal wine glass. 'Did you sleep?'

'Yes, thank you, to both questions,' said Caroline, and took the glass that Teresa offered her. 'I feel much better now.'

'Good. Dinner will be ready in about fifteen minutes. Shall we sit down?'

Caroline subsided on to the edge of an armchair and said: 'Would you like me to explain all this now?'

Teresa spread wide her hands. 'My dear, I must confess I am madly curious, but are you sure you want to confide in me? After all, we scarcely know one another.'

'None the less, I feel you're entitled to an explanation,' replied Caroline firmly. 'Also, I'd like to tell you.'

'Then do tell me,' exclaimed Teresa, smiling. 'I'm pleased you feel you want to tell me.'

'Well,' began Caroline, twisting her glass between her fingers, 'I met Adam in November, quite by accident, in the lift of the Steinbeck Building. I didn't know who he was then. I was a mere typist in the typing pool and I'd only been working there a very short time. I won't bore you with the intimate details, but to be blunt about it, we were attracted to one another at once. It was a physical thing at first, I think, but then it very quickly developed into something deeper. When I found out he was who he is it didn't seem to make any difference. I couldn't have cared less. To me, he's everything I've ever dreamed about.' She flushed and Teresa took a sip of her sherry, giving Caroline a moment's respite.

'Then about ten days after we met we went down to Slayford. Quite unexpectedly John arrived with a girl-friend. He wasn't pleased to find me there, as you can imagine, and I think he thought we were lovers. Anyway, a couple of days later Adam had to leave for America. Before he left I was sure he he loved me.' She sighed. 'But while he was out of the country, rumours started circulating about Adam and me. In the office, of course. You must know how damaging rumours can be and I didn't want our love to be turned into whispered gossip. Besides, Adam was the chairman of the Steinbeck Corporation and nothing like that had ever involved him before. Maybe I was stupidly naïve, I don't know, but when a boy from the office asked me out I thought it would scotch the rumours once and for all. I didn't know until afterwards he was the office Don Juan, or thought he was, anyway. He did try to get fresh with me, but luckily I got away. I hadn't enjoyed going out with him. All I could think about was Adam, and how soon he would be back.' She bit her lip. 'He came back all right. His secretary told him about me within five minutes of his landing, I think. Anyway, he came to my home on the Saturday evening and ended our association once and for all. He wouldn't give me a chance to explain. He made some excuse about me being too young for him after all. It was awful. . .' She broke off, her voice unsteady. When she had controlled herself again she said: 'I suppose it sounded bad to Adam. He must have thought I was only interested in him for his money and I wanted this other boy as a playmate. He treated me like some stupid child who can't decide whether he wants an ice-cream or a lollipop. So that was that! He went off to the West Indies, as you know, and it wasn't until January that I met John again.

'He seemed much nicer then and he certainly liked me well enough. I think at first I went out with him solely because he was Adam's son and I could keep in touch with Adam through him, unknown to Adam, of course. Then my Aunt Barbara died. She brought me up and was my only living relative. She left me twenty-five thousand pounds. You would have thought that would make a difference, wouldn't you? After all, I've never been used to being rich and I've always been interested in visiting foreign countries. But I'm afraid all I felt was completely rootless and alone. Scared too, if you like. Then John became very sympathetic and proposed. He begged me to marry him or at least become engaged. So I agreed. Don't ask me why. I must have been crazy. But this love I have for Adam seems hopeless now and I was too much of a coward to go on alone. Also, I knew if I gave John up I would sever all connections with Adam and I couldn't do that. Can you possibly understand?'

Teresa looked thoughtful. Caroline's story had explained everything, and she felt convinced it was the truth. It seemed too simple to be a lie. Surely if the girl had made it up she would have contrived some more complicated method of explaining away her association with this other boy. She could imagine Adam's hurt at Caroline's supposed defection, though. He was stubborn enough not to believe there could be any logical explanation. After his disillusionment with Lydia he was doubly unwilling to take anyone on trust. Besides, this girl was so young.

'How old are you, Caroline?' she asked suddenly.

'Eighteen,' answered Caroline with a sigh. 'But please, don't say I'm not old enough to know my own mind. I do, honestly. I love Adam. I've loved him for six months and I don't want anybody else. Last night when you rang I was attempting to compose a letter to send to John, finishing everything. I was going to Greece for a holiday and then I think I would have tried to see Adam just once more, to try and make him understand.'

'I see,' said Teresa, nodding, 'and what if Adam still refused to believe you, what then?'

Caroline shrugged wearily. 'I honestly don't think I could go on without him. Not for ever. It horrifies me to even contemplate such a thing.'

Liza came in, grinning as usual. 'Your dinner is served, ma'am,' she said cheerfully, lifting a little of the tension, 'will you come through?'

'Yes, thank you, Liza.' Teresa stood up. 'Give us a couple of minutes to finish our drinks.'

'Yes, ma'am.' Liza withdrew and Teresa turned to Caroline.

'Thank you for telling me all this, my dear.'

Caroline sighed, replacing her empty glass on the tray.

'What is your opinion, then?' she asked, hardly daring to voice the question.

Teresa looked compassionately at her. The story Caroline had told her had moved her tremendously. She was convinced that this child, she was little more in her eyes, might be good for Adam. And she wanted Adam to be happy; to live a normal life with a wife and family.

'I think,' she said slowly, 'that my son is a very stubborn man and that you must make him see reason. I think he is afraid that what you feel is only infatuation.'

'And you don't believe that?'

'No. I think you love my son.'

Caroline's eyes widened. 'And you don't disapprove?'

Teresa smiled. 'No, I don't disapprove. In fact, I should like to see Adam married, happily this time. His life with Lydia was never that. She was a rather miserable person, unable to envisage life on the scale that Adam was attaining. And now, I'm afraid, Adam believes himself to be self-sufficient. You are shaking his self-confidence. I hope you succeed. I wish you luck.'

'Thank you,' Caroline smiled tremulously. To know that his mother liked and approved of her was a wonderful feeling.

During the meal, Caroline enlarged upon her story. She told Teresa about her disastrous trip to Paris with John when everything seemed to fall apart. She skirted around his change of attitude towards her, but Mrs Steinbeck was shrewd enough to realise a little of what must have occurred. She already knew that John was a rather unstable person and the engagement had come as somewhat of a shock to her, knowing how he loved his freedom. She had supposed he was seriously in love, but in the face of Caroline's experiences it seemed highly unlikely. It was far more likely that John had surmised that Caroline was no loose young woman and the ties of an engagement might weaken her resistance. It was unpalatable but probable. He was very young for his years.

When they had finished dinner, Caroline, who had eaten very little, found her legs felt like jelly. She sat beside Teresa in the big saloon as Teresa drove to the large new hospital and dreaded the coming interview although nothing would have made her forgo it.

The hospital stood in its own grounds and commanded a view of Roseberry Sound. It was a modern, white-painted building that bore little resemblance to hospitals Caroline had visited in England. To begin with it was very futuristic in design with steel-framed windows and abstract-like ejections. She thought it looked more like an atomic research establishment than a hospital.

Inside, a lift transported them to the private ward where Adam was living. The long white corridors seemed endless and Caroline was glad of Teresa's reassuring fingers beneath her elbow.

'Don't worry,' said Teresa quite kindly. 'He can't eat you, dear.'

Caroline smiled nervously. 'No. He can't quite do that, can he?'

At last they reached the door of Adam's room and Teresa halted.

'Now, you go in,' she said firmly. 'I'm going to have a word with Sister. I'll not be too long.'

Caroline closed her eyes for a brief moment, praying for assistance.

'Oh, Mrs Steinbeck,' she whispered, 'I'm scared.'

'Go on.' Teresa leaned forward and opened the door, leaving it ajar. 'Buck up.'

Summoning all her courage, Caroline walked through the door and closed it behind her. She was in a room of generous proportions with wide windows opening on to a balcony. To her surprise, the bed was empty, and Adam was sitting in an armchair by the open windows. He was wearing a dressing gown over dark silk pyjamas, and studying some papers which he had taken from the briefcase on the table at his side. He did not look up immediately, and her heart plunged at the sight of him, so dear and familiar. His left arm and cheek were swathed with dressings, but she was relieved to see that his left eye was miraculously unharmed. Then he looked up and saw her, and the hot colour flooded her pale cheeks.

He thrust his papers aside, and stood up abruptly, his eyes dark and enigmatic.

'He—hello, Adam,' she murmured awkwardly. 'It's—it's wonderful to see you. How—how are you?'

Adam shrugged his broad shoulders. 'As well as can be expected, as they say,' he remarked regaining his composure. 'Why are you here? Is John with you?'

'No—at least—not yet.' She faltered. 'I—er—I got your mother's message, too. I've left word for John. I came at once.'

'Why?' Adam was coldly aloof.

'Why?' Caroline shook her head blindly. 'Why do you suppose?' She felt her voice quivering. 'Because

I was worried, of course. Because I didn't know how badly hurt you were!'

Adam's fists clenched. 'How charming!' he said, sardonically. 'You constantly surprise me, Caroline. Does my mother know you're here?'

'Of course. I went straight to her house this afternoon, when I arrived.'

'I see.' Adam glanced out of the window meaningfully, and Caroline felt a surge of rebellion rousing in her. He couldn't be as indifferent as all that. He just couldn't!

In truth, Adam's head was spinning with the unaccustomed exercise of simply standing, after several days in bed. He supposed the amount of drugs they had been doping him with were partly responsible, but the shock of seeing Caroline added its own strain.

As though realising he was not as well as he professed to be, Caroline quickly moved to him, looking up at him anxiously. 'Are you all right, Adam?' she asked huskily.

Adam tensed, looking down at her, his whole being pulsing with a desire so strong it was irresistible. 'No,' he groaned, his defences weakened by his illness and her nearness. 'No, I'm not all right at all.' He turned away, running a hand through his thick hair.

Caroline hesitated only a moment, and then she slid her arms round him, pressing herself against him. 'Adam,' she breathed, 'please. . .'

He turned then, unable to resist the temptation that was tearing him apart, and his mouth sought and found hers. Passion flared between them, they were hungry for one another, and his injuries were forgotten in desires of a more over-whelming kind. Caroline clung to him, subconsciously aware that she had taken advantage of his condition, and that Adam would not succumb so easily in the normal way.

When he put her from him, she was not surprised to find anger in his eyes. What hurt her most was the derisive expression he wore.

'Oh yes,' he muttered, 'this is very amusing isn't it?' He was bitter and hurtful, despising his own need of her.

'Adam,' she cried, 'don't be like this!'

'What should I be like? Polite, charming? I think not. Do you imagine you've succeeded now? Do you expect me to grovel at your feet? Is that why you got engaged to John? To create just this situation?'

Caroline pressed a hand to her mouth. 'Adam, I love you—'

'Spare me that, please,' he groaned in exasperation.

'It's true.' Her eyes were pleading, imploring him to believe her.

Unable to stand any more Adam turned abruptly away and sank down in his chair. He was still weak from the blood he had lost, and the knowledge that he wanted to believe her because of his own need angered him still further. How could he let her make a fool of him a second time?

Caroline, shattered by his words and not knowing of his inner torment, felt helpless. She stood where she was, trying to calm herself. It was almost with relief that she heard the door opening and Teresa came in.

Her sharp eyes sped from Adam to Caroline and then back to Adam again. She looked momentarily concerned.

With a bright smile she ignored the obvious tension and said: 'Hello, darling. Did seeing Caroline give you a surprise?'

'Yes, indeed,' remarked Adam dryly and lit another cigarette.

Teresa closed the door, frowning. Her anxiety grew as she saw how grey Adam was looking. The amount of blood he had lost would take a day or two to restore and although the doctors assured her he was making a steady improvement, it was apparent that seeing Caroline had been more in the nature of a shock than a surprise.

Twisting her gloves, she came to sit beside Adam, perching on the side of the bed while Caroline moved awkwardly to the door.

'I'll leave you alone,' she said quietly, her voice rather unsteady. 'I'll wait for you, Mrs Steinbeck.'

Teresa ran her tongue over her lips. 'All right, dear. I shan't be too long.' She noticed that Adam said nothing, nor did he look at the girl as she went out, closing the door behind her.

As the door closed, Teresa took a cigarette from the box on the side-table and helped herself to a light. Then she looked thoughtfully at Adam. He was lying back in his chair, his eyes half-closed. He appeared to be staring moodily into space.

'Well, Adam?' she said expectantly.

Adam opened his eyes wide and looked at her.

'Well what?' he asked harshly.

'Surely that's obvious,' exclaimed Teresa quietly. 'Adam, tell me truthfully, are you in love with that girl?'

Adam looked down at the glowing tip of his cigarette.

'I can't see that it's any business of yours,' he replied coolly, his voice polite but unapproachable.

'But it is,' exclaimed Teresa. 'You're my son and I want to see you happy.'

'And you think I would be happy with. . .her?' he mocked.

'Yes, I do,' cried Teresa angrily. 'Good heavens, man, can't you see she's in love with you? What have you been saying to her? She looked like a ghost when I came in.'

Adam did not reply immediately. He flicked ash from his cigarette into the brass ashtray and stared out of the window. He had no desire to discuss his affairs with his mother. Much as he loved her, he was not prepared to act like a lonely-hearts representative. Anything he decided, he had got to decide alone. No one could make the decision but himself. Dare he take the risk of Caroline meaning everything she had said?

'I think,' he said carefully, 'that I'm quite old enough to look after my own affairs. I don't want to hear any more about it, thank you.'

'But, Adam. . .'

He interrupted her, 'Have you heard from John yet?'

Teresa was infuriated but completely unable to force him to tell her anything. Adam had always been like this. Shutting up like a clam when his innermost feelings were involved. She could only hope he made the right decision.

'No,' she replied briefly, 'I haven't. I expect we'll hear tonight or tomorrow, though. I'm not worried. John will come when he's ready.'

After that their conversation was practically non-existent. Adam was absorbed with his thoughts and Teresa was too het-up to be able to relax. She felt bitterly sorry for Caroline and decided to cut short her visit so that she could comfort the girl.

'Oughtn't you to be getting into bed?' she asked, standing up at last.

'All in good time,' replied Adam infuriatingly. 'I expect I shall go to bed after you've gone.'

'Perverse creature!' exclaimed Teresa, and bent to kiss him. 'Goodnight, darling. Do look after yourself. You're the only son I've got.'

Adam smiled as she left. She really was incorrigible!

Caroline was waiting for Adam's mother in the visitors' lounge. She looked pale and withdrawn and they made the journey home almost in silence. Teresa felt desperately concerned for both Caroline and Adam. A storm was brewing in the air, and the sky hung heavily overhead as they turned into Roseberry Drive. Teresa commented on it and Caroline replied in a mono-syllable.

When they reached the house they found a taxi standing at the foot of the steps leading up to the front door. As Teresa parked the saloon a young man came running down the steps and stopped when he saw them. He had been going to get into the cab, but he came over instead.

'Why, John!' exclaimed Teresa, aware of the look of exhaustion that crossed Caroline's face as they both got out of the car.

John smiled at his grandmother. 'Hello, love,' he said, kissing her. 'I've just arrived and when Liza said you were at the hospital I decided I would go over and meet you. That's not necessary now, of course. How is Dad? Should I go and see him?'

Teresa bit her lip. 'I shouldn't go over right now,' she said. 'He's rather weary. He lost a lot of blood, but he's going to be fine. He has facial injuries, of course, and his arm is gashed, but none of them are really serious.'

'Thank heaven!' exclaimed John, studiously ignoring Caroline. 'I may as well pay off the cab, then.'

He walked away and Caroline and Teresa made their way into the house. Caroline's nerves were jumping. From John's manner she felt sure they were going to have a blazing row and she didn't feel she could stand it tonight. With each progressive minute it seemed to get hotter and she could feel the beginnings of a headache probing the back of her eyes. She supposed John was entitled to an explanation and she had treated him badly in one way, but after their upheaval in France she had felt sure he was growing tired of her. Tonight, after the scene with Adam, she only wanted to be alone, and the thought of her coming interview with John was nauseating.

Teresa led the way into the lounge and flung open both the doors. She dabbed her forehead with a cologne-scented handkerchief and said:

'My, but it's humid!' Then she turned and went back into the hall, calling, 'Liza!'

John came in as she went out and seeing Caroline, he at last spoke. 'Well,' he said coldly, 'what's all this about?'

Caroline ran a hand over her forehead. It felt hot and sticky. Her dress seemed to be clinging to her back and she longed for a cooling shower.

'I'm afraid I'm breaking our engagement, John,' she said quietly. 'Please don't make a scene. I don't think I could stand it.' She drew off the big emerald ring. 'Please, take this back. I'm sorry.'

John thrust his hands into his trouser pockets, belligerently. He ignored her outstretched hand and she was forced to hold on to the ring. All sympathy for her had vanished at her words and he only wanted to hurt her. She looked so beautiful standing there and she was the first woman who had ever rejected him.

'Indeed,' he said spitefully, 'and what am I to assume from that remark? Do I take it that my father is now back in the running?'

'Don't be horrible,' she whispered, wetting her dry lips.

'So it seems I'm right after all,' he taunted. 'My God, Caroline, you're taking a hell of a lot for granted! Just what do you think my friends will say about this? I'll be a laughing stock.'

'What am I taking for granted?' she protested bewilderedly. 'You knew in the beginning it was a gamble.'

'You're taking for granted the fact that I'll agree to release you from our engagement,' he replied smoothly.

'What can you do to keep me to it?' she demanded, and continued relentlessly, 'Where were you last night when your grandmother was trying to get in touch with you? Were you restoring your manly pride with some other girl? After all, as you said, you're not used to being turned down. What a shock that must have been to your pride!'

John was positively fuming. Caroline, now into her stride, made him appear like some stupid schoolboy. She certainly didn't pull her punches.

She pushed the ring into his hand and looked fearlessly at him.

'Let's have no more talk of that,' she said abruptly, as his grandmother came into the room. She was carrying a tray on which was a jug of iced lime juice and three glasses.

'It's so refreshing,' she said, setting the tray down on the table. 'Will you have some, Caroline?'

'Thank you,' Caroline nodded, and went to sit near the door. John also accepted a glass of the cooling liquid and flung himself into an armchair. He felt utterly fed up. Everything Caroline had said had been true. It was his pride that she had hurt more than anything else, although there had been a time when he had imagined himself in love with her. Her cool, blonde beauty fascinated him. However, it seemed it was not to be, and he was still outraged that she blatantly preferred his father.

Caroline now felt completely empty. She was glad she had got the scene with John over, but now there was nothing left. She didn't really have a reason for staying any longer. Adam had been so hurtful tonight and she was not John's fiancée any more. She had cut the ties with a vengeance, or more correctly, they had been cut for her.

After finishing her drink she excused herself. Her headache felt worse and she said she was going to lie down. Teresa was sympathetic and agreed that bed was probably the best place. However, when Caroline reached the seclusion of her room she felt very restless. She took three aspirins and wandered to the window, looking out without really seeing the view. She wondered achingly whether she might just as well return to London tomorrow. To stay would only make the eventual parting much more painful. She already liked Adam's mother; she didn't want to get any more deeply involved with her.

The humidity in the room was intense in spite of the air-conditioning, and Caroline, hearing the sound of the waves on the beach, longed to get out of the house. She had seen so little of this place and the idea of a stroll along the beach appealed to her. The storm was still threatening, but she didn't think it was imminent. Besides, the beach was only a few yards distant and she could hurry back if it began to rain.

Taking a cardigan with her, she left her room and walked along the landing to the top of the stairs. She could hear the voices of John and his grandmother coming from the lounge and she wondered whether she could get out without them seeing her. After all, she had no desire for further conversation with John tonight, and Teresa, knowing her troubled state of mind, might suggest that she accompany her. Much as she liked Adam's mother she wanted to be alone.

She crept quietly down the stairs, her low-heeled shoes in her hand. Half amused at the picture she must make, she quickly crossed the hall, passed the open lounge doors and reached the front door. Opening it silently she slipped out, just as Liza appeared from the kitchen. Her heart thumping, she stood waiting outside the front doors, hoping Liza had not seen her. When no one came she assumed she had not been spotted and putting on her shoes set off down the drive. She knew no one would see her here as the lounge overlooked the rear of the building. Feeling less like an

escaping criminal now she began to enjoy the unaccustomed breeze from the sea.

She saw no one as she walked towards the headland.
It was too late for the people who were dining out and
too early for those returning home as it was already
nearly nine o'clock. It was dusk, but the curious colour
of the sky shed a brilliance over everything. She didn't
feel scared. Storms had never frightened her.

She crossed the highway which ran along the cliff
top and reached the grassy slope which led down to
the beach. Two promontories curved out on either side
of the stretch of beach while the sand in the cove
looked white and undefiled. Caroline felt exhilarated
by the salty air and she began to descend the slope
slowly. There seemed no other way of getting down
and besides, the slope was very gentle.

Holding carefully to tufts of grass, and digging in
her heels as she went she moved down with ease. The
exercise banished all self-pitying thoughts from her
brain and she found she was enjoying herself.

And then, when she was within twenty feet or so
of the beach, the grassy slope gave way to a sheer
drop of bare rock. Horrified, Caroline remained where
she was clinging to the slope with urgent fingers. From
the cliff-top this drop had been hidden and she thought
in desperation that a warning ought to be given to
strangers like herself. Trying not to panic, she knew
that somehow she had got to get back up the cliff face.
It would not have been difficult if she had been facing
the slope, but she had gone down more or less facing
forward and now she was stuck, precariously above
the drop.

No wonder the beach had looked so clean, she

thought, furious with herself for being so foolhardy. Sighing, she glanced upwards. It didn't look so far and it was an easy slope. If she could just turn round she would be able to make it.

But fate took a hand, as it sometimes does, and as she attempted to turn, the heel of one shoe gave way and, with a startled cry, she felt herself plunging down on to the beach below. She landed on the sand, stunned by the fall, but within a few moments she was able to sit up and look around her. Luckily, the soft sand, had prevented her from breaking anything and she was soon standing up and looking up the cliff in exasperation. Now she had really done it. How on earth was she supposed to get back up there? The cliff face was completely sheer and even if she had been a climber she doubted whether she would have been able to get up it.

She sighed helplessly. She might even have to stay here until somebody found her, and on the heels of this thought came another, much more terrifying; no one knew she was out tonight. She might not be missed until morning. Suddenly she felt scared. There was very little likelihood of anyone coming along here tonight. It was getting quite dark now, and besides, the storm would deter people from leaving their homes anyway. Mrs Steinbeck would naturally assume she had gone to bed and was not coming down again. If only she had told them she was going out, instead of behaving like an idiot!

Suddenly she felt a spot of rain and there was an ominous roll of thunder. The storm was about to start. She looked around in desperation for somewhere to shelter, but although she walked from one side of the

cove to the other, there were no caves. It was a veritable prison, with no escape.

She felt utterly stupid and drew back against the
cliff face, trying unsuccessfully to keep dry. A flash
of lightning illuminated the cove and another crack of
thunder echoed menacingly. It was difficult to stop the
tears from gathering in her eyes, but she refused to
give in to them. It was no one's fault but her own that
she was in this position and she had got to make the
best of it.

It was about this time that she realised that the sand
beneath her feet was not the normal dry sand in a cove.
It was damp and firm and completely clean as she had
noticed before. That could mean only one thing; the
tide came right in, covering the cove completely and
thus making it unsafe to visitors. She went cold; she
had felt shivery before, but this was the coldness of a
petrifying dread. Was it possible she was to be
drowned regardless of whether she survived the night
in the open or not? She felt sick with fear. If only she
had never left the security of her room. If only. . .!
And how long before high tide?

CHAPTER NINE

IN the lounge, Teresa Steinbeck looked at her watch. It was nearly ten o'clock and she yawned sleepily.

'Dear me,' she said apologetically, looking at John. 'I must be tired. It's been rather an exhausting day.'

'Yes indeed,' murmured John moodily, stubbing out his cigarette. 'I think I'll turn in too.'

'Caroline must have decided to go to bed after all,' remarked Teresa casually. 'Poor child, I shan't disturb her. She's had a very exhausting day too.'

John did not reply. He and his grandmother had carefully skirted that topic of conversation for an hour and he had no wish to bring it up now. He was hoping to get to bed and leave all explanations for the morning.

Teresa stood up. She had noticed John's prolonged silence about his fiancée and refrained from making anything of it now. If he and Caroline had finished, then she would know about it all in good time.

Then, without warning, the telephone in the hall pealed shrilly.

Teresa stared at the noise. 'Good heavens,' she exclaimed. 'Who on earth can that be at this hour?'

Liza came along the passage and answered the telephone before Teresa could reach it. Teresa looked expectantly at her.

'It's Mr Adam, ma'am,' she said, holding out the telephone. 'He wants to speak to Miss Caroline.'

Teresa frowned. 'Now?' she exclaimed, taking

the receiver. 'Adam, is this a joke?'

'No, Mother,' came Adam's voice calmly. 'I just want to speak to Caroline.'

'Very well, dear, if you insist.' Teresa shrugged at John helplessly, but Liza looked perturbed.

'Has Miss Sinclair got back, then?' she asked, with the familiarity of an old servant.

Teresa put her hand over the mouthpiece of the telephone. 'What do you mean, Liza? Miss Sinclair is in bed.'

'Oh no, she isn't,' denied Liza, in her calm, unagitated manner. 'I saw her go out myself, not an hour ago. And I haven't heard her come back.'

Teresa closed her eyes momentarily as a multitude of thoughts swept over her. John leapt to his feet and came striding into the hall.

'Has she taken her luggage, Liza?' he asked swiftly.

'I didn't see any,' said Liza thoughtfully. 'But I can't be sure.'

'Oh, do go and see,' exclaimed Teresa agitatedly. 'Hurry, John!'

John ran quickly up the stairs and Teresa removed her hand from the telephone.

'What's going on?' exclaimed Adam, exasperated at the sudden dead sound to the telephone. 'Is Caroline there?'

Teresa bit her lip worriedly. 'Well, I'm not sure,' she began awkwardly.

'What the hell does that mean?' he muttered.

'Well...she went out about an hour ago,' said Teresa slowly. 'I...we...didn't see her go. John's arrived, you see, and we were talking in the lounge. Only Liza saw her going.'

Adam snorted angrily. 'Did she say where she was going?'

'No, Liza didn't see her to speak to. John's just checking to see whether her clothes are still there.'

John came down the stairs as she said this. 'They're still there,' he said, frowning. 'Where the devil can she be?'

Adam spoke again: 'Let me speak to John.'

Teresa shrugged and beckoned her grandson to the telephone. Reluctantly he spoke to his father:

'Yes, Dad. Are you okay?'

'Let's leave me out of it for the time being,' Adam muttered. 'What's been going on there?'

John hesitated and then said: 'Oh, you may as well know now. She broke our engagement. We had quite an argument, one way and another.'

Adam swore furiously. 'Is that why you were checking to see if her clothes had gone? Were you afraid she'd left abruptly?'

'Yes. . .hell, Dad, she may be out walking.'

'In this downpour?' exclaimed Adam sceptically. 'If anything's happened to her. . .' His voice was cut off as the telephone went dead.

John replaced his receiver and looked at his grandmother. She had gathered the gist of the conversation and was leaning against the door of the lounge.

'Well,' she said, 'so there was nothing to keep her here, then?'

John flushed. 'There was my father,' he muttered in a low voice.

'If you think she and Adam are together again, you're mistaken,' replied Teresa heavily.

'Then why. . .?' began John, in bewilderment.

'Why did she break your engagement? Oh, I think she realised after today that she couldn't marry you, and love your father. It was always a tortuous situation.'

John smiled moodily. 'I guess I feel responsible in a way, that is if she has left here for any other than valid reasons.'

'Don't even suggest such a thing,' exclaimed Teresa, shivering. 'Good heavens, she might be sheltering from the storm somewhere. But where?'

'That's the sixty-four-thousand-dollar question,' he replied. 'Well, I guess I'd better go and see if I can find her. Perhaps she's gone down towards the hospital.'

'What? When Adam has just rung from there?'

'Well, I'm baffled,' exclaimed John.

Liza shrugged her shoulders and made her way back to the kitchen. Teresa lit a cigarette with unsteady fingers and shrugged too. She couldn't help but remember Caroline's depressed condition when they left the hospital. The way she had placed so much emphasis on this interview with Adam. So much had depended upon it. Her rather strange words about life not being worth living without him assumed sinister proportions. Could it be possible that Caroline had disappeared purposely; maybe taken her own life? It just couldn't be true. She sank down on to a chair, feeling every one of her sixty-three years.

Meanwhile, John was pulling on his mackintosh. He buttoned it closely round his throat, trying not to consider what would happen if they found Caroline, injured or worse. He, of all of them should have shown consideration for her highly emotional state, but instead he had quarrelled with her.

Liza came back just then. 'I've looked in the grounds, ma'am,' she said carefully, 'and she's nowhere around.'

'Thank you, Liza,' said Teresa with a slight smile. 'You've done everything you can. Go and get your supper.'

'I ought to have told you when I saw the little lady going out,' said Liza mournfully, shaking her head.

'Not at all,' returned Teresa kindly. 'You weren't to know the circumstances. It's all right, really, Liza. We're sure to find her before long.'

Shaking her head, Liza returned to her kitchen, and Teresa rose to her feet again. 'Well, John,' she said, 'where are you going first?'

John shook his head. 'I honestly have no idea.'

'What about the cove?' exclaimed Teresa suddenly. 'It's natural that she should be drawn to the beach. It always looks so inviting.'

John frowned. 'Surely not? Hell, Grandmother, she would see the notice warning people. She couldn't go down there. Besides, how would she get down?'

'The notice doesn't stretch the whole length of the cliff top,' retorted Teresa irritably. 'I've always said what a dangerous place that was. As for getting down, maybe she fell, like a few others have done.'

John looked unconvinced. 'It's a bit far-fetched, isn't it?' he said, frowning.

'Oh, for goodness' sake,' snapped Teresa angrily, 'stop arguing. Go and find out.'

John thrust his hands into his trousers pockets and walked towards the door. 'You don't think we ought to call the police?' he said thoughtfully.

Teresa lost patience. 'No, I do not!' she cried furiously. 'What could we tell them? That a friend staying here is out for a walk and should be back by now? Sounds rather feeble, doesn't it? Or would you rather I told them that we were afraid she might commit suicide?'

John flushed. 'All right, all right, I only asked,' he muttered, and opened the door. As he did so there was a squeal of tyres on the gravel drive outside and Teresa put her hand to her lips.

'The police!' she breathed, hardly aware of moving to the door.

The sound of footsteps rang on the steps and the door was flung open. Adam came in, dressed in a dark overcoat, shaking the drops of water from his curly hair. Fully dressed now, he looked powerfully dependable standing there and with a cry Teresa ran to him and hugged him. 'Oh, Adam,' she whispered, 'I'm so glad you've come. We're so worried. How on earth did they let you out?'

'I discharged myself,' replied Adam briefly, looking over her head at his son. 'I gather you haven't found her yet?'

John moved uncomfortably. 'I was just going to look,' he said.

'And where do you intend looking?' asked Adam curtly, turning up his coat collar as his mother straightened up away from him, composing herself. 'I've a cab outside. We may as well use that. It's pouring down.'

'Grandmother suggested the cove,' said John. 'Do you think it's worth a try?'

Adam frowned. 'Why there?' he asked, turning to his mother.

Teresa clasped her hands nervously.

'Caroline was in a very depressed state,' she explained. 'When we left the hospital this afternoon she didn't seem at all herself. . .and. . .'

'Do go on,' muttered Adam angrily. 'What else?'

Teresa shrugged. 'Surely you can guess what I'm afraid of?'

Adam frowned. 'You mean suicide? I don't believe it. Not Caroline.'

Teresa shrugged.

'Maybe I'm over-sensitive,' she offered.

'I think perhaps you are,' said Adam, but his face had taken on a taut, worried look. Then with sudden decision he continued: 'Right, we'll try the beach. What time is it? High tide covers that strand. If she was to get caught there at high tide it wouldn't make much difference what her intentions were. Have you got a rope, John?'

John shook his head. 'Grandmother,' he exclaimed, 'a rope. Have you got one?'

Teresa paled. 'Oh Adam! Why should I need a rope?'

'A clothes-line, then,' muttered Adam impatiently. 'Hurry, Mother. We may not have much time.'

They eventually took Liza's plastic-covered clothes-line and ran out to the cab. Adam ordered the driver to hurry. It was only seconds to the cliff-top, but every second counted when they didn't know how long they had.

Caroline's courage had long since deserted her and she remained unhysterical by a great feat of will-power. The tide seemed to be coming in so fast and it wouldn't be long before it covered the sand where she stood.

Already rivulets were forming on either side of her and she pressed back against the hard cliff face as though she expected the wall to give way and save her. She had been shouting on and off for such a long time and her voice was quite hoarse. She had known that there was little point in it really as no one had passed along the cliff top, but she had had to try to satisfy herself that she really was alone.

She wondered whether the water would be deep enough to drown her. How deep was it at high tide? Of course, the force of it eddying around might sweep her off her feet and if that did happen it would be just as bad. She could swim, but not against a tide that might sweep her against the cliff, and the headlands on either side were too far out to swim round. Besides, even if there were no strong currents in the Sound, there might be nothing beyond the headland but more rocks and she might not be able to get back again.

It was torturing to realise that there were people and houses only a few yards away from the cliff top. Could it possibly be that she was to die here only a few steps from Adam's house?

She was soaked to the skin already and more frightened than she had ever been. What would Adam think of her when he found out? Of course, she thought bleakly, she might not be around to find out. Her trip to America had not proved a very great success one way and another.

The storm had passed over, but a heavy drizzle was now soaking her anew. She felt cold outside but colder still inside. She thought how wonderful it would be to be able to shelter somewhere and maybe even dry herself with a warm towel.

When she heard the car coming she thought she was imagining things. Its headlights swept the cliff and the car came to a halt. She stared in disbelief and then stiffened, panic-stricken, as she felt sea water oozing round her ankles.

As though in a daze she heard men getting out of the car, talking. Summoning all the energy she could find, she shouted as loudly as she could: 'Help, please, help me!' and burst into tears.

They heard her and looking up she saw the silhouettes of two men outlined against the headlights of the car.

'Caroline!' shouted a voice, Adam's voice. She surely must be dreaming all this. Adam was in hospital.

'Adam,' she croaked, her voice giving way, 'I'm down here!'

There was a moment's silence and then he shouted: 'Okay, honey, hang on. We've got a rope.'

Within a few moments, the longest moments of Caroline's life, a loop of plastic clothes-line came down to her. Caroline caught it, her fingers cold and fumbling.

'Got it?' called Adam. 'Right, now, put it round your waist. It's a slip-knot and it will tighten as we begin to pull you up. Try and hold on to the line and take some of the weight off your body, okay? When you reach the grassy slope, you'll be able to walk up with the help of the rope.'

'All right, Adam,' she said hoarsely, and did exactly as he asked. The line was strong and secure and it only took a minute to bring her up. She could hardly believe she was standing on the cliff top again. She looked a sorry sight, wet and bedraggled, her hair straggling round her face, her eyes wide and frightened still, naked fear showing in their depths.

John released the rope from around her waist and looked shamefacedly at her, but she looked at no one but Adam.

'Caroline,' he groaned, his voice gruff with emotion. 'Oh, you crazy little fool,' and he pulled her into his arms, uncaring of her wetness, pressing her close against him, warming her a little with his body. His injured arm was forgotten and the cab driver and John walked tactfully away.

Caroline clung helplessly to him. It had been worth all the fear of the last hour to feel his arms around her again and to know he cared.

'You came,' she whispered brokenly. 'You came.'

'Of course I came,' he groaned softly. 'God, Caro, don't ever do a crazy thing like that again. I've been half out of my mind with worry.'

Caroline merely pressed closer against him and regretfully he put her away from him and led her to the car.

'You're saturated,' he muttered. 'Come on, you need a hot bath before you catch a chill, or pneumonia.'

It only took seconds to reach the Steinbeck house. Adam, ignoring the pain in his arm insisted on carrying her indoors and up to her room. Caroline protested that she could walk, but he paid no heed to her words.

Teresa was in the hall, pale but thankful, and instructed Liza to hurry ahead of them and turn on a bath for Miss Caroline. Adam stood Caroline down in the bedroom and said:

'Right, strip off,' in a commanding tone, which brooked no argument.

Wondering wildly whether he intended to supervise her ablutions, Caroline began to unbutton her cardigan, sliding it off her shoulders. However, Adam walked to the door as she did so.

'I'll be back later,' he said, his eyes dark and fathomless. Then he slammed the door behind him leaving her alone.

The bath was very hot, but Caroline found herself enjoying it and her whole body relaxed luxuriously. After the strenuous evening she had had it was balm to her aching limbs. Liza helped her into bed afterwards and she slid thankfully beneath the silk sheets. Then Liza went away to heat some milk for her.

Soon after she had gone there was a light tap on the door and Caroline's heart somersaulted rapidly. 'Come in,' she called expectantly, and then was half disappointed when Teresa entered the room. She walked over to the bed, looking thankfully at Caroline. It was wonderful to see her here, safe and well.

'My dear,' she exclaimed, seating herself on the edge of the bed, 'what a dreadful shock you gave us all! What on earth possessed you to go down there?'

Caroline looked apologetic. 'I'm awfully sorry to have caused you such concern,' she apologised, 'but I really didn't intend to do so.'

'Didn't you see the warning notice?' asked Teresa.

'What warning?' exclaimed Caroline. 'No, I'm afraid in the half-light I must have missed it. You see, I was keeping one eye open for the storm. I didn't want to get caught in it.'

She laughed, half-nervously, remembering her ordeal.

Teresa shook her head. 'Thank heaven you're safe!

I'm always advocating for a fence to be put along there, but mostly the sign deters strangers.'

'I've been very stupid,' said Caroline, sighing. 'I think it's a habit with me.'

'Not at all,' protested Teresa, smiling. 'Accidents will happen. We're only too happy to know that nothing worse happened to you.'

Caroline smiled and put her hand over the elder woman's. 'You're very sweet,' she said. 'I'll never be able to thank you for being so kind to me.'

'Nonsense,' exclaimed Teresa deprecatingly. 'Besides, these things all happen for a purpose. Perhaps it has done some good after all. Maybe it's brought someone to his senses.'

Caroline understood her meaning. 'How did Adam come to find me?' she asked suddenly.

'He discharged himself from the hospital,' replied Teresa, shaking her head. 'He was very concerned. I've never seen him so perturbed about anything.'

Caroline twisted her hands together. If only it were true!

After Teresa had departed, she lay back against her pillows re-living those moments when Adam had found her. Then, with practical determination, she put those thoughts from her mind, and picking up her hairbrush began to brush her hair. Liza came back with her hot milk and some aspirins and insisted on seeing Caroline take them.

'There now,' she said, satisfied when all the milk had gone. 'You'll feel much better in the morning. My old clothes-line surely did come in handy.'

'That it did,' said a voice from the doorway, and Caroline looked up, her pulses racing, to see Adam leaning against the jamb watching her. He now had his arm in a sling but looked big and handsome, dressed in dark slacks and a sweater.

Liza went out chuckling and Adam closed the door firmly. Then he said: 'Well, now who's the invalid?'

Caroline flushed. His nearness always disconcerted her and she felt the disadvantage more strongly because she was in bed. However, as he advanced towards the bed she saw that his eyes held warmth and affection and she felt her body tingling in anticipation.

'I'm sorry to have caused such havoc,' she murmured softly. 'I'm such an idiot.'

He smiled indulgently, not contradicting her.

'Will your leaving the hospital make a lot of bother?' she said anxiously. 'I mean, you haven't had your stitches removed, have you?'

'No. I'm staying here tonight and I report back there tomorrow.'

Caroline twisted her fingers together. 'Will you get into trouble?' she asked uncomfortably.

'I hardly think so,' he replied lightly. 'You see, I sit on the hospital board of directors.'

'Oh.' Caroline felt foolish. She ought to have realised that men like Adam Steinbeck did not have to behave in any constricted pattern.

'And how do you feel?' he asked softly. 'I hope you haven't caught a chill. It was lucky we found you as we did. High tide was only about fifteen minutes away.'

'I know,' she shivered. 'I was petrified.'

'With good reason,' he said soberly. 'That cove is very dangerous. That's why it's never used. My mother tells me you didn't see the sign.'

'That's right. Oh, Adam, how did you find I was missing?'

Adam smiled, and sat down on the side of the bed.

'Fortunately I telephoned you at about ten o'clock and that was when you were found missing. Liza had seen you go out, but of course she had attached no significance to it.'

'So she did see me.' Caroline sighed. 'I wasn't trying to do anything silly, as your mother suspected. I simply wanted to be alone. John and I—we'd had a row, you know.'

'Yes. He told me,' Adam nodded. 'That was why Mother was so upset.'

'She's been so very kind and understanding,' said Caroline, smiling faintly. 'I really think she likes me.'

'So do I,' remarked Adam casually, 'which is just as well, as she's going to be your mother-in-law.'

'What—what did you say?' Caroline couldn't believe her ears.

'I'm asking you to marry me,' said Adam quietly. 'God knows, I need you badly enough.'

Caroline's eyes were as wide as saucers.

'That's why I rang you from the hospital,' he went on, caressing her fingers with his. 'I wanted to tell you, right then. I couldn't risk your leaving without seeing me.'

'Oh, Adam!' she exclaimed. 'I can't believe you mean it!'

With a muffled exclamation he leaned forward and pulled her into his arms. 'Then I must show you,' he murmured huskily, and proceeded to do so, his mouth finding hers in a long absorbing kiss. Caroline wound her arms about his neck, holding him closer, unwilling to let him go. But Adam became aware of how little she was wearing, and of how easy it would be to lose control completely.

'When will you marry me?' he demanded, a trifle thickly. 'It's got to be soon. As soon as I can get a licence?'

'Oh, yes,' she breathed, her face flushed with his lovemaking. 'Oh darling, you do believe I love you?'

Adam smiled. 'Of course. I'm glad you didn't give up. I'm glad you came out here. I've been a fool.'

'Have you?' Caroline bent her head. 'What—what about Mark Davison?'

He shrugged his shoulders. 'I'd made up my mind this evening that whatever the consequences I must have you,' he said heavily, pressing her fingers to his lips. 'But while you were bathing, just now, my mother told me the true story, as you'd told it to her.'

'I see.' Caroline looked up. 'If only you'd let me tell you!'

'I know,' he said, shaking his head. 'But jealousy is a terrible thing.'

'Don't I know it?' exclaimed Caroline, clasping his fingers tightly. 'You were so stubborn.'

'I know. And so much time I've wasted. But I promise we won't waste any more.'

Caroline smiled tremulously. 'I'm glad you had the accident,' she whispered shyly.

Adam grinned. 'Now there's a thing to say!' he teased her, and then at her expression, he took her into his arms again.

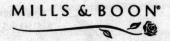

Back by Popular Demand

COLLECTOR'S EDITION

A collector's edition of favourite titles from one of Mills & Boon's® best-loved romance authors.

Don't miss this wonderful collection of sought-after titles, now reissued in beautifully matching volumes and presented as one cherished collection.

Look out next month for:

Title #19 **The Shrouded Web**
Title #20 **A Trial Marriage**

Anne Mather

Dangerous Temptation

He was desperate to remember... Jake wasn't sure
why he'd agreed to take his twin brother's place on
the flight to London. But when he awakens in hospital
after the crash, he can't even remember his own
name or the beautiful woman who watches him so
guardedly. Caitlin. His wife.

She was desperate to forget... Her husband seems
like a stranger to Caitlin—a man who assumes there
is love when none exists. He is totally different—like
the man she'd thought she had married. Until his
memory returns.
And with it, a danger that threatens them all.

"Ms. Mather has penned a wonderful romance."
—Romantic Times

1-55166-269-8
AVAILABLE NOW IN PAPERBACK

MIRA

MILLS & BOON®

Anne Mather

COLLECTOR'S EDITION

If you have missed any of the previously published titles in the Anne Mather Collector's Edition, you may order them by sending a cheque or postal order (please do not send cash) made payable to Harlequin Mills & Boon Ltd. for £2.99 per book plus 50p per book postage and packing. Please send your order to: Anne Mather Collector's Edition, P.O. Box 236, Croydon, Surrey, CR9 3RU (EIRE: Anne Mather Collector's Edition, P.O. Box 4546, Dublin 24).